THE HUNT

J.M. DABNEY

DAVIDSON KING

Hostile Whispers Press, LLC

ISBN-13: 978-1-947184-25-1

Edits by Stephanie Carrano

Cover by: Five Star Designs (Morningstar Ashley)

Cover content is for illustrative purposes only. Any person depicted on the cover is a model.

REMEMBER:

This book is a work of fiction. All characters, places, and events are from the author's imagination and should not be confused with fact. Any resemblance to persons, living or dead, events or places, is purely coincidental.

PLEASE BE ADVISED:

This book contains material that is only suitable for mature readers. It may contain scenes of a sexual nature and violence.

AUTHOR'S NOTE

This story contains scenes of extreme depictions of trauma/violence. Some readers may find objectionable.

I dedicate this book to my insanity. It's a familiar friend that likes to come out and play every so often. Thanks to JM Dabney it seems to be sated for the time being. Without my insanity my writing would be boring.
- Davidson King

This book is dedicated to all the readers who take a chance on my words and appreciate the characters created in all their forms. And thanks so much to Davidson King for sharing the characters we created. Davidson made this an amazing experience.
- J.M. Dabney

PROLOGUE

RAY

The sickening odor of decomp attacked my senses as soon as I walked through the apartment door. I'd almost ignored the call altogether, thinking it was my captain wanting to chew my ass out for the fourth time. Him ordering me around, while it amused me occasionally, it also pissed me off. I was a cop before the fucker had lost his virginity in the backseat of his daddy's car.

I stepped out of the way of the chaos, uniforms loitered beside the door as the forensic teams scoured the room for clues. The M.E. gave me a dirty look, and I grunted as I slipped on those damn booties. As I closed the distance, I dug out my old school notebook from the inside pocket of my wrinkled blazer. I wasn't one that went much for dress codes, but again, I'd already gotten my ass reamed for supposedly messing up.

There was no way I fucked up evidence. I'd done this job way too long for that to happen. I shoved the problems to the back of my brain to focus on the situation at hand.

"What you got for me, Donnelly?" I asked as I squatted next to the dead body.

Young kid, probably in his early twenties and nude.

"In my gut, Ray, we got number three. Same M.O. except this kid has been lying here for few days at least. Our guy doesn't usually let a body go unnoticed. Doesn't stroke his ego enough."

"I saw the press. They get here before us again?"

"Crowd control was a nightmare."

"So, tell me what you got?" I posed my pen over the lined paper.

Donnelly lifted the thin bloody sheet to show the lower half of the victim's body, exposing the mutilated genitals. They looked to me as if the assailant had crudely removed them. It was a detail none of us had released to the press, and I had to agree with Donnelly that it looked like we had a serial.

The Brass always turned squirrely when anyone mentioned serial killers. It wasn't as if I wanted to deal with all that bullshit. Serials always brought the nutcases out of the woodwork and the FBI sticking their noses in. I wasn't one to work well with others. My Captain hadn't assigned me a long-term partner in years.

"The genitals were removed, but as with the other two victims that was done post-mortem. The facial injuries were, as far as I can tell, done first. The extent of the rage in these attacks has to prove as least some type of history between—"

As Donnelly went through the play by play, I took notes, and I couldn't deny this was too like the previous scenes. Same victim profile. Rage at this level always meant the victim knew the assailant.

"Does he have the same club stamp on his wrist?" I asked.

Donnelly ran the light over the kid's inner wrist to expose the photochromic ink. Club Epiphany was popular with the college party crowd. A pretty mixed crowd of gay and straight, I'd shown the kids' pictures around and received no information. I could see the lies in their drink-hazed gazes, but I hadn't pushed too much.

"Call me when you're ready for the post-mortem."

"Will do, Ray."

I straightened and grimaced at the sound of my creaking knees. Maybe I was getting too old for the damn job. I roamed the apartment. I made my notes and jerked my attention toward the door as someone yelled my name. A snarl curled my lips and widened my nostrils as I noticed the Captain waiting in the open apartment door.

Fucker, he was just there to bust my balls. Captain Green was a slick bastard. The suit he wore was more than I made in a month. I couldn't say Green was dirty. I didn't have concrete evidence, but I'm sure he wasn't maxing out his credit cards to pay for his lifestyle. Rumors were rampant that Green had himself a pretty boy on the side.

I raised my hand and waved him off, I wanted to finish the walkthrough before I had to deal with him.

I didn't fault him for the side piece. I wasn't in the closet by any means, but I didn't flaunt it at work. No matter how progressive the modern police force pretended to be, I still had to have my fellow officers watching my back.

The stupid thought caused me to shake my head. I was well past my prime, and I existed on a cop's salary. I didn't even want to think about the last time I had a man in my bed. Hell, I didn't even remember the guy's name.

I talked with a few cops to procrastinate, yet that wouldn't save me for long. Getting it over with would be best. I skirted the edges of the room.

"Captain," I greeted him as I came to a stop.

"You have a meeting with Internal Affairs in thirty minutes. Get a move on."

The sudden announcement made me momentarily stupid and then my anger took over. I didn't need this fucking bullshit.

I'd never once stepped over the line. I prided myself on being a good cop.

"What the fuck are you talking about?"

"You'll do as I say."

Everything in me wanted to argue, but it was already a shit move for Green to inform me on the crime scene. I wasn't going to cause a scene.

"I have a post-mortem to attend. I don't have time for this shit."

"If you don't want to deal with it, Detective, you know what you can do."

The bastard would come in his pants if I ever handed over my badge and gun. I already had over twenty years in and didn't know how to do anything else. My fists clenched as I slipped out of the door and jogged down the steps to my unmarked car.

Not until I was locked inside did I let out the string of curses and roughly turned the key in the ignition. I didn't know why Green had it in for me. My file was full of commendations, and I'd made it to this point in my career by good police work.

I jerked the car into reverse and backed up, then shifted into drive to make the half-hour trip downtown. My brain formulated every worst-case scenario. I was a pessimistic son of a bitch and I knew it. You didn't work sex crimes and homicide as long as I had and not turn hard.

Life didn't let you travel the easy route, especially how I'd started out. I wasn't always a cop, hadn't always walked the straight and narrow, but an old beat cop had straightened me out. Since then I made the law my life, and I.A. starting to fuck me without the courtesy of lube pissed me off.

Weaving through traffic, I made it back to the department in record time, and before I parked, two familiar faces were waiting for me. Sims and Marlowe, two hard-assed cops from Internal

Affairs, were standing in front of my car. I got out of the driver's seat and slammed the door.

"Was this fucking necessary?"

"Don't want you running, do we, Detective?" Sims sneered.

They made a show of taking positions, Sims in front and Marlowe behind me. The stares were a heavy weight as every cop focused on the spectacle I.A. was making of me. Like I was already guilty.

I was led into an interrogation room. Marlowe played big and bad by posting himself beside the door. His arms crossed over his chest as he glared at me.

"Have a seat," Sims ordered, then threw a file on the table.

It wasn't like I had much choice, so I pulled out the chair and took a seat. No way was I going to give these bastards the upper hand. I hadn't made it this far by being a pushover to kids playing cops and robbers.

Sims took his time opening the folder and reading the contents. It was almost laughable that they were pulling that Interrogation 101 bullshit with me. They weren't going to make me sweat with their amateur move.

"Let me begin by making it clear this is an official interrogation. You have the right to have your rep here, and I suggest you take advantage of a lawyer. Charges are being filed as we speak."

I clenched my teeth so hard my jaw hurt as I stared at the smug bastard seated across from me. In my gut I knew this wasn't going to end well if they were already informing me of my rights. Maybe I should've replied or taken the offer of a lawyer, but didn't that give the impression of my guilt? I hadn't done anything and I wasn't going to act as if I had.

"Detective Clancy, can you explain the ten-thousand-dollar deposit made into your account a week ago?"

"What fucking deposit?" I surged forward.

"Two days after evidence on your case was *misplaced* a deposit was made. Can you explain that?"

"That's bullshit. I ain't taken a bribe in my life. Have you seen my file?"

Outrage burned hotter in my gut at the scam Sims was playing. My evidence and confessions were above reproach.

Sims turned a few more pages. "Mixed in with those commendations there's quite a few reprimands for excessive force. Your clearance rate on your cases is outstanding. Twenty-five percent higher than anyone else in the department."

I barely restrained the urge to bring my fist down on the table. "Don't even question my record. Every one of those was a clean collar. Perps love to scream police brutality when they're going down for life or getting death sentences. I ain't dirty, Sims."

"Then how do you explain the money that made it into your personal account?"

"Do you think I would be dumb enough to put that money in? I've been a cop long enough—"

Sims slammed his hands down on the table top. When he didn't get a reaction from me the man's jaw clenched. I'd spent more time in an interrogation room than on the streets. I knew every trick and if they were idiotic enough to think I'd make a mistake like that then they weren't as good detectives as I'd thought.

"You're dirty, Clancy, and we're going to prove it. We've been cleared to ask for your badge and weapon. You're on leave without pay and if it's up to us, we're going to lock you up where you belong."

"This is bullshit. You've got nothing on me, but a bogus deposit. Check the cameras, you'll see I didn't make that deposit."

Sims removed a grainy photo from the file and slid it across the table. The figure I studied was similar in height and build. Dressed as I would be if I was off-duty. That wasn't me, but with a cursory examination it was a classic case of mistaken identity. Who the fuck had it out for me? Like any cop, I've had a few collars threaten payback, but that amount of money, no one I knew had those funds and that amount of animosity. Or did they?

Sims brought his index finger down on the image as if to emphasize the accusation in his cold brown eyes. "The cameras picked up a man looking just like you. If you just confess, you can make it so much easier on yourself."

"What and put all my cases up for review and possibly have the convictions overturned? You're stupider than I fucking thought. I'm not dirty. I don't take bribes. I can say it slower if you can't comprehend."

"Turn over your badge and service weapon, Clancy."

I surged to my feet knowing that I wasn't going to get anywhere. Arguing wasn't going to change their mind. They had a sudden hard-on for me and I didn't know why. I removed my sidearm and placed it on the table, then unclipped my badge from my belt. The table rattled with the force that I slammed it onto the scratched surface.

"Do we have to warn you not to leave town?"

The sneer on Sims' face made me clench my fists as the urge to beat the arrogance out of the younger man overtook me.

"Marlowe will escort you to your locker."

One more degrading act to top off my night. As I exited the room, a file box connected with my abdomen and my hands clenched around it so tight the sides caved inward. I wouldn't show anyone else that I was breaking inside. Everything I'd worked for in almost two decades shattered around me.

Someone had pulled one hell of a frame job, and the problem was I didn't know why. I knew I wasn't liked, but I sure as fuck was respected. I ignored the curious looks and the whispers as I made my way to the locker room. My hands shook with rage as I packed the few personal items I kept in the small space into the box. All this was bullshit and it was too easy, how didn't anyone other than me pick it up?

If they thought I was going to let this stand, they were dead wrong. I'd figure it out and I'd rub their accusation in their faces. I wasn't dirty. I knew who was and sooner or later I'd get enough evidence to take them down and maybe, just maybe, get my job back.

1

ANDY

On a good day I was just glad my socks matched, that any holes in my clothes weren't so revealing I scared a small child or a sweet grandmother. The fact my work outfit was more than four months of rent made me constantly nervous.

I began working at Augustine's three years ago as a busboy. I was the oldest busboy at twenty-five but was hopeful the owner would see something in me and give me more opportunities. That happened almost two years to the date of hire when one of the servers came down with the measles, and there was a huge party coming into the restaurant that evening. Augustine told me I had to serve, he never asked, always demanded. He threw a suit at me that was too big on me, which wasn't shocking, told me to wear it and do a good job.

I had never worked so hard in my life. That night I was on point and when the evening ended, Augustine gave me a card to his tailors, told me to get fitted, and to be back the next night as a server.

Now I owned three suits all paid for by Augustine. Two thousand each. It was my responsibility to make sure they were clean, crisp, and hole free.

Francis, my roommate, always laughed at me when I would come out of my bedroom and walk to the front door because I practically skirted around the room. I couldn't afford replacing even one suit, and it was made clear to me if I ruined one I had to replace it. I was paid very well working at Augustine's, but so many years of not getting a decent paycheck had forced me to take out loans and credit cards I couldn't afford.

My busboy paycheck was next to nothing and went to bills, rent, and minimum payments on my cards and the loans. After working as a server, I was just now out of debt and had opened a savings account. Francis and I were destined to move out of our shitty place and into a better one. I figured another two years and we'd be looking back at all this and laughing.

I'd just entered Augustine's for my shift when I was greeted with a very irate sommelier. Gabin was cursing at Augustine in French, swinging his arms around and stamping his foot. My boss leaned against the doorjamb of his office with a bored expression. They'd been together for twenty years and had married three weeks after it became legal to do so in this country. Their fights were legendary and the staff often found them amusing. But Gabin was truly livid this time.

"Trouble in paradise?" I whispered to Elise, one of the other servers.

"Oh yeah. Gabin caught Augustine in bed with Trenton, the new bartender. Apparently, it happened a few nights ago, but Gabin was off, so when he came in today he saw Trenton working the bar and well..." She gestured to the couple in question.

"Wow." I was both intrigued and saddened by this news. I loved Gabin and Augustine together, to hear of something like this broke my heart. I was a sucker for a love story and theirs was one that deserved a happy ending.

"You're in the Crystal section tonight," Elise said as she

lightly patted my arm. "They could be at this for hours; we better rock tonight or Auggie will likely fire us in a fit of rage." She wasn't wrong, we'd seen it happen.

Augustine's was always booked. You had to reserve a table at least six months in advance and attire was just on the cusp of formal.

Whenever I walked through the doors it was like stepping onto a stage. I had to put on a performance, play my part, because the real Andy Shay liked to sit on his couch in his mismatched socks, hole covered clothes, and play video games with Francis most nights. I bought food that was on sale and shopped at Goodwill. At Augustine's I was Andrew Shay poised and proper. No holes, no mismatching, all smiles and sophistication.

"Welcome to Augustine's, my name is Andrew and I will be your server this evening. May I offer you a cocktail, aperitif, or beverage?" This was how I greeted all customers. I had to look up what an aperitif was when I started working here, and I Googled a lot, too. I had no idea if Gabin would be doing his sommelier duties tonight, but I couldn't let that concern me right now. If they wanted wine, I'd have to figure it out.

It turned out being a stressful night. Gabin did work but not until an hour into food service. Trenton was fired and I was sure some sort of lawsuit would come from that. Elise was forced behind the bar leaving me my section and hers to cover. My feet were throbbing, my back ached, and the headache dancing behind my temples was sure to be a doozy by the time I trekked home.

"Need a ride?" Elise asked as we stepped out into the clear night.

"Nah, I can still catch the bus and after tonight, I just want to pop in my ear buds and decompress."

She waved me off with a tired smile. I didn't hate my job, but

I didn't love it. It was a job that paid my rent, kept the lights on, got me out of debt finally, and put food in my belly. It paid higher than a fast food joint, and the tips were way better, but unfortunately, I couldn't live in the section of the city I worked. Not yet anyway.

I lived on top of a laundromat with my roommate, Francis. It was four rooms. Two bedrooms, a kitchen, a tiny living room, and then we shared a bathroom. We each paid three hundred toward rent, split the bills, and it was a bonus we liked each other.

It was also a perk that we were roughly the same size. He was far prettier than me and not all elbows and knees, but we were close in measurements. So, we shared clothes and often our closets were a mix of each other's.

The bus stop was a few blocks from the restaurant, so the walk wasn't that bad. I took a relieved breath when I got on the bus and saw it was mostly empty. No chance of a crazy lady wanting to talk about her cats or a man asking if I could help him find his teeth.

With music in my ears, I leaned my head against the cool glass and watched as the scenery turned from posh to poor.

The bus stopped across from my place, and I dragged my weary body to the door and wasn't shocked when it stuck. With what little energy I had, I pulled it open and winced at the smell of mold. This place should probably be shut down, but then where would I be? Sure we could get a better place right now, but we didn't want to settle. We wanted to be able to live not worrying that if we lost a job we'd be forced right back here.

There was no elevator, but fortunately it was only a flight of stairs to climb. The music made the dreariness of the building a little more bearable, and when I reached the apartment door, I almost cried with joy.

Joy turned to confusion when I went to push the key in the

lock, and it opened without me turning it. Immediately, I pulled the buds from my ears.

"Francis?" Probably not a great idea shouting his name, but for all I knew he had someone over and was fucking on the couch. We usually hung a sock on the door if we had company, and the lack of a sock sent a jolt of fear through me.

"Francis?" I yelled again as I so very slowly pushed the door open.

The apartment looked normal. No signs of distress, and when I peered around the corner to the kitchen, the light above the stove cast a welcoming glow. Francis often left it on for me when I worked late so I wouldn't bang into things. My clumsiness wasn't something either of us enjoyed.

I figured Francis either forgot to lock the door or there was something wrong with the lock. I turned to return to the front door to shut it when a crashing noise came from Francis' bedroom.

"You ok?" I yelled. There was no response, just a thud.

Shit. He probably fell. Drank too much and was fucking around and fell. I quickly shut the front door and rushed to Francis' room.

"I'm coming in so get as decent as you can in your drunken state, asshole."

I opened the door with a flourish, ready to tease the shit out of him when I stopped dead in my tracks. It was like my limbs seized up and fear owned my entire body. Francis lay on the ground naked in a pool of blood. His eyes, gone, something was carved into his chest, and... oh god... his penis. I wanted to shout, scream, run to him. I couldn't—I was locked in place.

I heard hangers clang in his closet and everything inside urged me to run. Whoever did this was still here. I had to call 911. I knew Francis was dead, but I had to call for help.

It wasn't until Francis' closet door burst open that I was able to feel my legs. The killer. I couldn't see their face, only their eyes. They were covered head to toe in black, and there was a medical bag hanging from one hand. It was the vicious looking knife in the other that had me backing out of the room.

Run, Andy, fucking run. My brain was screaming and finally the rest of me caught up, and I made for the door as fast as I could. I heard the springs on Francis' bed, so I knew he jumped on the bed and I was being pursued. I hadn't locked the front door, so as soon as I opened it I began shouting for help.

Footsteps behind me had my heart racing and in my clumsiness, I tumbled down the stairs. My back slammed against the wall at the lower level, and when I raised my eyes, the killer was at the top of the stairs. Staring at me. *Fuck.*

"Help!" I frantically rose and pulled on the door. Stuck. Goddammit! "Someone call 911." It was a piece of shit neighborhood and no one wanted the cops around, but maybe someone would come out of their building.

The killer began rushing down the stairs just when I got the door open. I pulled out my cellphone as I ran down the street still calling out for help.

"911 what's your emergency," the dispatcher asked.

"My roommate, he's dead, killed, I'm being chased down Chopsey Avenue toward Don's Café. Please help me."

"Calm down, sir, get to the café it's twenty-four hours. I will dispatch a car there, and what's your address where you live? I will have cars and an ambulance sent there."

I was quickly running out of breath, but I could see the lights of Don's ahead. When I looked over my shoulder, I saw the killer was still chasing me.

"I live above Tumble Dry Cleaners, apartment one."

"Police are en route, are you at the café yet?"

I'd just entered the café when she asked. There were a few patrons who all turned to look at me when I entered.

"Just got here."

"Are you still being pursued?"

I sat at the furthest booth and searched the night through the window. Nothing. No one was there.

"No, they're gone."

"Okay, sit tight, police will be there in two minutes. Please stay on the line...."

It was all I could hear. Everything was catching up with me. Francis was dead, mutilated. Fear and despair battled in my chest. With my head in my hands, I began to sob. No one paid me any mind. Why would they? I don't know how long I sat there crying, but I knew there was one question I needed to figure out. What the hell was I going to do?

2

RAY

I shoved a book under the leg of my desk; I swore the floor started to sag more every day. Six months had passed since I took that bullshit deal the D.A. offered so that I could keep doing what I was good at. He'd told me I could take an early retirement and leave quietly. The one thing a D.A. doesn't want to deal with is having every case his office tried come under scrutiny. I never thought I'd see the day where I had an office with Ray Clancy, Private Investigator on the door in a building one foundation crack from being condemned. New West City wasn't a booming metropolis, but it had all the cesspool dynamics of a big city.

It wasn't like I'd ever be out of business but following around cheating spouses most of the time wasn't my idea of a good time. To be honest, it barely paid my bills. If I wasn't careful, my shitty office would become home sweet home.

I pushed a sigh through my compressed lips and reached for the bottle of antacids. After I twisted off the cap, I shook several onto my palm and popped them in my mouth. I chewed them and chased them with cold coffee. Whether it was my morning cup or the one from last night, I didn't know and personally didn't care.

Replacing the cap, I made sure it was tight and tossed it back on my desk. The contents rattled as the container rolled across my desk and onto the floor.

I rubbed the growing curve of my stomach. Luckily, it was still firm, but I was feeling and looking every one of my forty-five years. Hard living had taken its toll. It was there in the harsh angles of my face. The multiplying silver at my temples that stood out starkly against the dirty blond of my hair.

With a deep growl, I pushed up from my desk and grabbed my jacket on the way to the door. Analyzing my looks wasn't something I did.

I jogged down the creaking steps and out onto the busy sidewalk. When I reached the curb I looked both ways, then ran across the street to the diner. Rudy's was a staple of the neighborhood, frequented by criminals and cops alike. I opened the door and stepped into the rundown restaurant. The place was a mixture of decades. My gaze swept the room, I nodded my head at Finn Mac and a few of his enforcers glanced at me but went back to their meals. Mac ran the Irish Syndicate in the city. He had his fingers into just about everything except he didn't deal in flesh or drugs.

I couldn't fault Finn. Criminal or not, he always stood behind his word. I couldn't say we were friendly, but we'd developed a civil acquaintance. I respected his skewed moral compass. I didn't know what that said about me as a cop or a human.

I took an empty seat at the counter. Rudy poured me a coffee without being asked.

"How ya doing, Clancy?"

"Doing, man."

Back in the day, Rudy had briefly walked the beat, but after his old man Rudy, Senior had a heart attack, he'd left to run the diner.

"You seen the paper?"

"Not yet, I was following some woman for her husband. I'm running out of room on a page for the men she visits." I slipped two fingers through the handle of the mug and raised it to my mouth. A sigh slipped free at the strong, bitter brew.

Rudy pulled a paper from under the counter and laid it in front of me. I set my mug aside and picked up the newspaper, unfolding it to catch the headline.

Has a Serial Killer Made New West Their Home?

That got my attention and I scanned the article. Harry Simpson was a long-time crime reporter for the New West Gazette. The man had some shady contacts. I shook my head at the vague details, but what was there was too much like the past repeating itself. The killer went quiet when I'd gotten kicked off the force, but it seemed they were back to the grind.

It wasn't my business. I no longer had a badge, but my fingers itched to get my hands on the official file. Every cop had that one case that went unsolved, and this looked to be mine.

"What're your thoughts?"

"No longer my place."

"We both know that's a lie. You gotta have one helluva hard-on because," Rudy tapped his finger on the black and white page, "no cop likes to have an unsolved."

I folded the paper and handed it back. "Doesn't matter whether I like it or not. I'm not a cop anymore."

"Keep it, you can read it later. Once a cop, always a cop, you know that as well as I do."

"Isn't my business." It was a lie and I knew Rudy picked up on it.

The killer was going after innocent kids. Kids, I snorted, when did I start thinking of twenty-somethings as kids? Just another clue that I was getting old. But my age didn't matter, what mattered was I knew in my gut that the cops weren't anywhere near figuring it out. Those pictures of the before and after, the files and reports still haunted me. Not just for the fact that I couldn't finish it, but that this guy wasn't going to stop.

He didn't leave any evidence behind. Everyone left a trace of themselves wherever they went, but this guy was smart enough to cover his tracks. The only hope was he'd make a mistake.

"Want your usual?"

"Yeah, I got time for something to eat before my client's wife gets off work."

Rudy jotted down my order, and then turned to attach it to the spinning holder in the small order window. The older man wandered off to refill coffee mugs and wait on a couple who'd just walked in. As I let my mind wander, I lazily sipped my coffee.

I knew guys that loved this private investigator shit, but I wasn't one of them. My pride stung that I was mostly following around cheating spouses. Sneaking around in the bushes taking pictures. I was caught between wanting my job back and being bitter over the way I was forced out. My attention kept straying to the article, and I set my mug down so quickly the black liquid sloshed a bit over the rim.

I picked the paper back up and quickly unfolded it. That time I read every word. Looked for clues between the lines, and the Brass was denying there was a serial killer. I still had my notes, and suddenly wanted to run back to my office to read over them.

Other than the type of victim, the only other link was Club Epiphany. The suspect had to be young. Someone in their late thirties or forties would stand out. I reached into the inside pocket of my jacket and dug out my notebook.

I wrote down some notes. It wouldn't hurt to ask around. I

hoped I still had a few friends left on the force. Another project to focus on would break up the monotony of my carbon copy cases.

"Not your business, huh, Clancy?"

I raised my head and shook it at the big man's amusement.

"Fuck you."

"How many times I gotta tell you, Clancy, you ain't my type."

Rumors ran rampant no matter how big or small the city, and it wasn't a secret I was gay. I was surprised when it wasn't a big deal.

"Good, because you ain't pretty enough for me," I said with a smirk.

Rudy snorted as he leaned his hip against the counter and crossed his arms over his wide chest. "So, talk it out."

"The higher ups are continuing with their bullshit of this not being a serial. If these are related to my last case, this guy isn't going to stop."

"True. What else?"

That's what frustrated me the most. Warnings made people more aware of who they encountered and remaining quiet kept the victim pool deep and clueless. They hadn't even released names or photos of the victims, and it seemed they were going to keep up with the same bullshit this round.

"THEY SHOULD ISSUE A WARNING. I MEAN, FUCK, THESE YOUNG MEN have no clue who they might be taking home."

"Why do you think he's picking them up? Could just see them. Tail them for a while and strike when the opportunity opens."

That was a plausible theory and at first, I'd agreed with it, but these kids were street smart. Survived by their gut instinct.

"Hypothetically, if this is the same unsub as before. There's no evidence of forced entry."

"Man, what about entry points? Some people get too damn comfortable, leave windows unlocked. With enough skill any lock can be picked."

All my theories had the what-if flaws. I shouldn't even be thinking about this case. I knew it was going to come back to bite me on the ass.

"Yeah, but my experience tells me that this guy loves the game. Just striking when their defenses are down would be way too easy."

A bell chiming ended our conversation and I put my stuff away, my usual of a burger and fries was placed in front of me. I doctored my food with hot sauce and tried not to think about the heartburn that was sure to come later.

"You're getting old, Clancy. Should start taking better care of yourself."

I grunted as I took my first bite and ignored him until he left.

I had an hour before I needed to be across the city to start tailing my current case, but my brain was occupied with the more interesting prospect of a New West serial killer. They hadn't come up with a flashy name for him, yet. I knew it was only a matter of time before they branded him like some celebrity.

It might turn out to be a mistake, but I needed this. I wanted back in the action even if I was on the outskirts in a civilian compacity. I made mental reminders to call in a few favors. My fingers were crossed that I had a few allies in the department. I didn't understand my compulsion, but as with every aspect of my life, I played it by instinct.

3

ANDY

My body felt like I was hit by a truck. My bones ached, my muscles were sore, and my head pounded. The nurse who looked me over said it was due to adrenaline and how my body had initially locked up.

Between the police and the hospital, I wasn't released until the next day, late afternoon. There weren't many people I could call for help. Normally I'd ring Francis, but...the thought caused a lump to form in my throat, and my heart felt like it was shredded. It was a jarring feeling to know someone was dead, someone you loved like a brother. I sat in that hospital bed staring at the ceiling remembering all his smiles. The good morphed into bad as I wondered how much pain he must have been in. That led to more tears and eventually vomiting.

I was nervous calling Elise since I'd never really asked her for anything before. We were work buddies, not friends. But she didn't hesitate, and without me wondering where I was going, she took me to her apartment. I was so zoned out I never got a chance to really see the outside of the place.

We didn't speak much, she said she wasn't sure what she could say to make this even a little bit okay. The inside of her apartment wasn't much bigger than mine, but it was in a safe part of town, and she decorated it to feel like a real home.

While I showered she set up her couch, called Augustine and explained everything, and he told her to relay his deepest condolences and to take the week to grieve. Of course, that made me worry more. There was no way I could go back to my place; the killer saw my face. The police treated it all like I stumbled upon someone stealing my underwear, not carving into my friend.

I knew in my heart there was no way I'd be able to ever be in that apartment again. It wasn't like Francis got sick and died in the hospital. He was murdered in the place he should be the safest. If the fear of being in there didn't get to me, the utter depression would.

Exhaustion got the better of me and before I knew it, I was fast asleep. The smell of sauce and spices woke me, and the view out Elise's window was dark. Night time. I'd come to fear this time of day. As a kid we believed monsters were under our beds or hiding in our closets, parents taught us that was silly and we trusted them. But monsters are real and they are in our closets and—

"You awake?" Elise's voice was soft and the sound of her footsteps shook me from my dreaded thoughts.

"Yeah, just thinking."

She sat beside me, worry and sympathy shown in her cornflower blue eyes. "Your thoughts aren't a safe place to be right now, Andy." Gently, she took my hand in her own. "I don't have a roommate or anything. You can stay here as long as you need to. Don't let that be something else worrying you."

"I heard one of the cops talking at the station; he said the killer carved words into Francis' chest and stomach." The pounding of my heart echoed in my ears. I didn't want to repeat them; at the same time, I didn't want to know it all by myself. "Said he wrote 'Come Back To Me' in his skin."

"Oh, Andy." She pulled me close and wrapped me in her arms. I was tall and lanky and Elise was small and plump. It wasn't a graceful hug, but it was one I didn't realize I needed until her warmth thawed the chill of fear.

"Who would do that to Francis?" The tears flowed, and my already raw throat began to close. "What does any of it mean?"

"I don't know sweetheart and I have nothing to compare it to, but you know what I do know?" She scratched the nape of my neck, and it felt nice to be comforted.

"What?"

"I know how to get through sadness. I made spaghetti, meatballs, and garlic bread. I picked up a triple chocolate cake at the bakery by work, and there's a rom-com marathon on Lifetime. I say we stuff our faces and cry it out with Reese Witherspoon and Julia Roberts."

Suddenly my sobs were replaced with laughter. It wasn't going to fix anything, the fear was there, but Elise wanted to help me forget for a night and I wanted that, too.

"Sounds perfect. What can I do to help?"

We spent the next hour filling our faces with delicious carbs and then sat on the couch, each with a huge slice of chocolate cake, and began our movie marathon. At around eleven I looked over and noticed Elise was fast asleep. I grabbed the remote and changed the channel to the news. There had to be something on there about Francis. And while just thinking his name made my pulse ache, I couldn't pretend it wasn't real.

It wasn't until twenty minutes into the newscast that they began to talk about it.

"What we have been able to find out is Francis Darby was brutally murdered in his apartment over Tumble Dry Cleaners last night. Police are tight lipped on this case, but a source at the police department told me it was similar to the murders six months ago. Of course, when questioned Captain Green offered 'no comment,' and it has us all wondering if there's a serial killer on the loose, and what does this mean for the young men of New West City?"

I couldn't hear anymore, hitting the button the living room was immediately washed in darkness and silence.

"What happened?" Elise jolted awake. "I fell asleep. Damn, I'm sorry."

"No, it's okay. It's late. You should go to bed. I'm going to wash up and pass out myself." I didn't want to tell Elise what I just saw because I didn't want her panicking on top of everything else.

She hugged me good night and when her bedroom door closed, I turned the side lamp on and reached for my phone. I Googled everything I could find on the murders six months ago. There wasn't much which was a little concerning, but one in the New West Gazette went into detail about the killings. It sounded exactly like Francis' death. Words were carved into the bodies, but the reporter wasn't able to find out what exactly. Going through the archives I found an article from two months ago, same reporter, wondering what ever happened to the killer. He spoke about his sudden disappearance speculating he left town or was killed himself.

I knew from reading this that the killer was back and for some reason, Francis was his latest victim.

Scouring both articles, I searched for anything that could help. A name, a location, someone aside from the reporter who knew and would believe me that I was in serious danger.

Captain Green appeared often, but another name was repeated almost as much. Detective Raymond Clancy. He was lead on the case before the killer disappeared. I wondered if he would be taking over again since the murderer was back?

Doing a search for him didn't give me much with the police force. I wondered if he'd retired or quit? I scrolled a little more, eventually finding Raymond Clancy, Private Investigator. There was a number and address. It was too late to do anything about it now, but first thing in the morning I was calling him.

I wasn't able to shut the light off beside me, and I checked and double checked all the locks in Elise's apartment. I knew the killer saw my face and I'd told the police. They had told me they would have a police car drive around Elise's apartment, and to let them know when I started back to work and a police presence would be there.

It was the most concern I'd seen from any of them. How could they not be more caring that my life was in danger, that I'd just witnessed the only person in my life that mattered slaughtered before my eyes? A quick glance of my clothes answered that question. They likely saw me as a poor guy, not important to society. Not realizing I was a man saving for a better life. To them I was barely worth the man hours. Well, I happened to like living and wanted to do it for at least another seventy years. Tomorrow, I'd call this Raymond Clancy and see about him swapping some information and maybe, if I was really lucky, he'd help to keep me alive.

4

RAY

I scrubbed my tired eyes as I entered the Medical Examiner's Office. It was morbidly comforting to be in a familiar place. The scents of antiseptic and death bringing back memories. I missed my old life. Since it was still early the staff was at a minimum, but I knew Donnelly practically lived in his office.

Strolling through the halls, I checked the windows into each autopsy room and when I didn't find him, I made my way to his office. The door was slightly ajar, and I felt my lips pull into a grin at the sight in front of me. Donnelly's head tilted back with his hair sticking up in all directions and his glasses crooked as he snored..

"We don't pay you to sleep on the job," I yelled as I pushed the door open to bang against the wall.

Donnelly was on his feet and straightening his jacket before he realized it was me.

"You bastard." Donnelly cleared his throat. "What the hell are you doing here?"

"Your new D.B. and don't tell me you can't talk to me."

"Have I ever said I couldn't?"

"Nope." I walked into the room and plopped down on the chair with its peeling and cracked vinyl seat.

I waited while Donnelly retook his seat and leaned forward to place his forearms on his desk. When I'd left the force, I'd told myself I would keep in touch with friends. That was until I no longer had my badge and I wasn't part of the club anymore. The friends I'd thought I had turned out to be nothing more than acquaintances. That made life lonely as fuck.

"First things first, how you doing?"

I was getting tired of that question. How am I doing? Every answer I had would turn out to be nothing but a lie. Although, the truth wasn't much better. "I'm good. Exciting life of a P.I. and all that."

"You fucking hate it, Ray. I know you do or you wouldn't be here wanting to snoop."

"Same guy?"

"You don't lead up, just go right in for the kill. Learn a little foreplay, maybe that's why you're still single."

I snorted and rolled my eyes; I didn't want to talk about my sex life any more than I did how I was doing.

"It's similar."

"Don't make me have to pull teeth."

"First instinct, same guy."

Donnelly was a thirty-year veteran of the M.E.'s office. I'd trusted his gut plenty of times over the years.

"Can I get a look at the report?"

Donnelly didn't wait before he tossed the autopsy finding across the desk. I grabbed the file and studied it slowly. It was easy enough to see the case matched the ones I'd worked, but the killer seemed to have left the job undone.

"He's never been this sloppy before. Facial disfigurement. No signs of sexual abuse. The removal of the penis wasn't done this time, but it seems he was in the middle of doing it.

What happened?" I finished reading the file and wanted to get my hands on the case file so bad but knew that wouldn't happen. I closed the folder and placed it back on Donnelly's desk.

"Interrupted. Kid's roommate came home from working late. Word is the kid ran. Killer chased. He hid out in some twenty-four-hour place." Donnelly spoke as he stood, and I watched him pour two cups of coffee.

"Do you know the kid's name?"

"Not a clue. Upstairs is being hush-hush. The brass' asses are so tight they couldn't fart if they wanted to, and it's only going to get worse. I don't know why the guy stopped, but—"

Donnelly turned back to me and stopped talking as he handed me the chipped white mug.

"But what?"

"Did you ever think about the coincidence of the killings stopping when you were kicked off the force?"

I hadn't, killers got caught for different crimes or moved on to another city. Maybe waited for the heat to die down if they thought someone was getting too close. It wasn't unheard of for a serial to go underground for years, decades, and then restart.

"It hadn't. Who says he stopped? Maybe he changed his M.O. or moved on."

"Could be, but you're being obtuse. Let's play What-If."

Donnelly didn't look like a man well into his fifties when he got that slightly maniacal youthful glee at the prospect of playing armchair detective. The man had my back and let me look at the file, the least I could do was play along.

"I hate that fucking game."

Okay, I wasn't going to concede gracefully.

"You love it and it feeds my Detective Envy, so do it."

"Fine." I took a sip of my coffee and waited for Donnelly to start his favorite game.

"What if he went underground because you weren't on the case anymore?" Donnelly asked.

"Then shouldn't there have been more personal messages from him? Gifts? Letters sent to the precinct or left at the scenes?" That was the big thing. If the guy wanted to draw me out, wouldn't there have been more contact outside the murders and just hoping I showed up to investigate? I never felt like a target.

"He was only three murders into his spree. Unlike you, maybe he knows what foreplay is."

"Could we just leave my skills out of this conversation?" At this point I was so out of practice I wouldn't know what to do with a man if I had him in my bed. People loved dating cops, Badge Bunnies were a thing and I'd had my share. I gave my head a rough shake at my thoughts.

"Did I hit a nerve, Ray?"

"Let's move on, next what-if."

"What about the new part of the M.O., the words carved into the chest. 'Come back to me.'"

"Maybe a copycat. Someone who knows some of the details. Cops with loose lips talking in public and someone wanted to take out an ex, and the best way to do that is frame another killer."

"You're not making this fun for me."

"I didn't think that was part of the game."

"I'm being serious here, Ray, what if he's back for you? That you're his actual target."

"Wouldn't his victims look like me? Similar build and age, not twenty-something kids. And the club, the blacklight stamps for Epiphany. That's his hunting ground. That's a place I don't go and never have, except for a few times for the case. Harlon Gadsby, the owner, and his husband are the only ones I spoke with."

Gadsby was about my age. Married with a husband half his age and the husband managed Epiphany. Both the men had been more than helpful when I'd spoken with them. I hadn't gotten that creepy vibe off either of them. The two men seemed very much in love. You could tell a lot about someone from their body language. The two men had hovered near each other as if gravity pulled them together. I'd quickly marked them off the suspect list.

"I still think it's something to consider whether you think it's farfetched or not."

"Sorry, Donnelly, I don't see it. If there was some evidence that he was calling me out then I'd agree, but at best you made a circumstantial case."

"Men have been sentenced to death on nothing more than circumstantial evidence."

I remained silent as I finished off my tepid coffee, and then leaned forward to set the mug on his desk. I straightened and realized I had more questions than answers, but this was as far up the chain of command as I could go. Green wasn't going to let me anywhere near the case, and as fucked up as it was, cops who worked serial cases were territorial. Finding a serial killer was newsworthy, got your name in the headlines. Famous by association.

"Would you keep me in the loop? Just let me know if another body comes in."

"Will do, I'll ask around and see what I can come up with for you."

"Who do they have on the case?"

I asked in the hopes it was an acquaintance, maybe someone who owed me a favor.

"Green took lead last night. I don't think anyone has been assigned yet. As far as I know, they're still working it as a completely unrelated case."

I had no doubt that more bodies would start showing up. Then a piece of information from earlier came to mind, there was a witness. Possibly a roommate or boyfriend of the victim, that made me wonder if they'd put him out in the cold. I doubted Green would be human enough to assign protection. I made a mental note to pick up a paper on my way back to my office.

"I appreciate the help, Donnelly. Being friends with me could be career suicide."

"No, Ray, they fucked you over with that case. You'd made plenty of enemies. Even I saw that frame job a mile away. You were a good cop. I never doubted that."

My chest tightened, not many people had defended me, but it was nice to hear someone who believed I was innocent on my character alone.

"Thanks, man."

"No problem. I still got your number. If I hear anything, you'll know it."

I nodded and said my goodbyes. The walk back to my nondescript, shit colored car was made at a slow pace as I went over the details in my head. I lifted the handle and grimaced at the grating creak of the hinges. Everything around me was falling apart, my car, my house, and the building where I had my office. It wasn't anything new, six months ago, my life had spiraled.

I got into the driver's seat and jerked the door closed. Luckily, my car still ran like it was new, and I made my way across the city to my office. When I exited my car, I made sure to grab my camera to print off the newest set of pictures. I'd worked the case for two weeks, and there was more than enough evidence to prove my client's wife was fucking around.

Maybe my client got off on being cuckolded. Everyone had their kink. As long as my client's checks kept clearing I'd take the money. Right now, my pride wasn't as important as having a place to live. That thought depressed me and I ran up the steps to my office, using my key to unlock the door. When I entered, I kicked the door closed and tossed my camera on a nearby chair.

I dragged a large corkboard from the corner and positioned it in front of my couch. I made quick work of starting a timeline. Using printer paper, I drew large question marks to indicate the killer, newest victim, and the unnamed witness. I found my old notebook and wrote down more facts on paper to tack them to the board.

By the time I was done, I had the basics and hopefully, with Donnelly's help, I could fill in more in the days to come. Like always, I knew there would be more, but how many more? That's what terrified me. How many had to die before the department would get their heads out of their asses?

I took a seat in my office chair and opened my laptop to start researching. I needed to do a national search to see if the killer had stopped or prove Donnelly right that the guy was after me. If that were true, then I had the blood of those young men on my hands for some reason only known by the killer.

These kids had died for something I'd done or at least the killer's perceived wrong that I'd perpetrated. I hated the unknowns and what-ifs. This was up to me to solve, if the killer was after me then this was my problem. I couldn't let another young man die because of me.

5

ANDY

Waking up in Elise's apartment would probably be disorientating if I'd slept at all. I think I dozed for a few minutes here and there, but mostly, I found myself staring at her cream-colored ceilings trying to figure out what it entailed to change my name, face, everything.

It was clear the police didn't care much about my safety and I was on my own. I should've paid more attention in gym class that week they taught self-defense. I guess I was going to have to figure it out. The pep talk gave me about two seconds of positive energy, then Francis' face popped into my head, *"Andy, is that my holey Superman shirt you're wearing or yours?"* I was hearing his voice in my head. I missed my best friend so much.

I waited until Elise left late in the morning to call that P.I. I found in the news article. I hoped so hard he either knew something that could help me or maybe he'd help me himself.

An odd thought hit me right before I pressed send, *what if the P.I. is the serial killer?* I mean anyone could be, right? My bus driver, Augustine, Gabin? Oh my god, I was going to drive myself crazy.

I was out of options, if he was the killer, then I was making a huge mistake. If he wasn't, then I stood a fifty-fifty chance of surviving this.

Breathing deeply, I hit send and pressed the phone to my ear. One ring. Two rings. *Maybe he's not there?*

"Ray Clancy, Private Investigator." The sound of his voice both startled me and sent a shiver of lust through me. It was gravely like he was a smoker but sexy like silk. "Hello, anyone there? I don't got time for this."

Oh right, I need to speak.

"Hi... uhm, I mean hello my name is Andy I... well I got your number from an article, right?"

"Are you asking me?" Ray asked, a hint of annoyance laced his sarcastic tone.

"No. Sorry. I'm nervous."

The sigh the investigator released was loud in my ear, and I began to feel complete dread. No one was going to help me in this shitty city.

"Look, I get whatever you have to say makes you nervous, but I don't know if I can help if you don't use your words." There was a warmth there, but I could tell he was likely ninety percent asshole. I didn't need a nice guy, I just needed one who would help me stay alive.

"I think someone is trying to kill me." My words came out jumbled; I hoped he was able to understand what I said.

"I see." There was a rustling on the other end, sounded like papers. "Your name is Andy. Do you have a last name?"

Ray didn't seem at all shocked by my word vomit confession and maybe that was good. Or bad.

"Shay."

"Andy Shay. Okay." More rustling. "Shit, where the hell is my pen?" Now there was banging, cursing, and then silence.

"Mr. Clancy?" I asked wondering if we were disconnected.

"Yeah, here. Couldn't find a pen. I'm good now. So, Andy Shay, why do you think someone is trying to kill you?"

"Well, he chased me and I sort of witnessed him killing someone. Hence the chasing. And so, I get the impression he or she isn't someone who wanted to be seen, again, hence the chasing. I was able to call the police and hid at Don's Café until they arrived. They have a car on me, but it's not always there and..." Listening to all this out loud, I sounded like a loon.

"Wait. You witnessed a murder?" Again, the sound of papers filled my ears.

"Yes, my roommate." I couldn't say Francis' name without bursting into tears, and I was sure this investigator thought I was insane already. No need to solidify that with uncontrollable tears.

"Holy hell. You're the roommate." He said it like it was a revelation. "The murder above the laundromat." He wasn't asking me. He heard about it. As seedy as this city was, Francis' murder was brutal enough to have everyone talking.

"Mmhmm. Yeah. Look, I know you're not a bodyguard or anything, but I was doing research after the news said this happened before. Anyway, your name came up and—"

"Yeah, few months back. I was on the force then. Look, would you be willing to come to my office, or if you feel better, we can meet somewhere public. We should talk." The gravely assholishness seemed to have disappeared and genuine interest, and maybe tenderness, laced his tone. I didn't think he was the killer, but I still wasn't meeting him alone with no witnesses.

"I'd rather meet in public if that's alright?"

"I get it. You know Rudy's Diner?"

Everyone knew Rudy's. Francis had lived for his Reubens. "I know it."

"Can you meet me in about an hour?"

Looking at the clock I saw it was after the lunch rush, so it wouldn't be overly crowded, but enough people would be there so if I was murdered there would be witnesses at least.

"Yeah, okay, one hour. I have to catch the bus; I won't make it if I walk, and to be honest, walking anywhere right now isn't safe for me."

"I'll head over there in a few. Is this your cell you're calling on?"

"Yeah."

"I'll text you my cell number. If you run into any problems, just text me where you are. Got it?"

Was it odd I liked that someone would come running if I was in trouble? "Sure, okay."

"What do you look like?" Ray asked, and it was the type of question I hated. How does someone describe themselves?

"Uhh, tall I guess, lanky, dark hair... nothing special. Just look for the guy pissing himself, that'll be me."

His chuckle eased the tight coil in the pit of my stomach. "Will do."

He hung up without a goodbye, and I hurried to the bathroom for a shower. Like every shower in existence, I crouched under the spray to wash off. A half-hour later, cleaned, brushed, and dressed, I hopped on the bus toward Rudy's.

Where I would normally pop ear buds in and stare out the window, I found myself too paranoid to daydream. It felt like everyone was looking at me. *Was the killer on this bus? Are we passing them on the street? Can he see me through the glass?*

I saw Ray had texted me his cell number, and I hoped I wouldn't need it because I was drowning in a pool of my own blood. *God, I was dramatic.*

I took a second to drop a message with Elise that I was meeting someone who may be able to help and that I'd message her when I was on my way back. She asked if I'd grabbed the spare key, and I was glad I had, because she said she was closing at the restaurant.

The bus stopped and I waited until I was the last person to exit. There was something about not wanting to be stabbed in the back.

Rudy's was directly across from the bus stop. I took a deep breath and raced across the street. Opening the door, I searched out the place. It took me a second to figure out who Raymond Clancy was.

His eyes were staring into a coffee mug, and while I couldn't see the color, I just knew they were dark. His hair was mostly gray, but under the fluorescent lights golden strands peeked through. He was a worn-out man, but there was no way I wouldn't jump him if he offered.

When he looked up, those brown pools held a lot of emotion. He knew I was who he was waiting for, and I knew he was a man who had seen more shit than what I was running from.

6

RAY

Rudy had given me a strange look when I'd walked in a few minutes earlier and didn't take my usual spot at the counter. I was still mentally processing the call I'd received from one Andy Shay. I'd done a quick search for him and found several social media profiles from different Mr. Shays, but didn't take the time to do a more thorough investigation.

When he'd stated he'd witnessed a murder, I'd resigned myself to dealing with another crazy person, but then after Andy had explained, my tired brain had quickly put the pieces together.

Andy sounded young and justifiably scared. His voice was soft with slightly husky notes. I didn't know why out of everything the kid's voice is what I remembered most.

I raised my mug to my mouth and downed half of it, hoping the caffeine would wake me up. I should've slept. I'd spent most of the morning researching and hadn't come up with one mention of similar crimes. Even if there was only one detail the same, I'd grasped at hope, only to be disappointed when the suspect was dead or imprisoned. I don't know how I felt about that, but I didn't have time to think too much about it.

I curved my hands around the mug and stared into the dark liquid. The bell going off over the door had me lifting my head. A thin man walked in with clothes that hung on his frame. As soon as I'd looked up our eyes met. There was no doubt in my mind that he was the one I was waiting for, and I slid out of the booth. I sensed the young man's fear, so I patiently stayed still as he prepared to approach me.

Andy's first few steps were cautious, as if he hadn't made up his mind on whether I was an ally or foe. I knew that expression, I'd lost count of how many times I'd seen it over the years. Two decades of dealing with terrified and reluctant witnesses prepared me for anything.

"Mr. Clancy?"

I was slightly taken aback by the sound of that voice in person and blamed it on my lack of sleep. The kid was young, maybe mid-twenties.

"Call me, Ray. Please, take a seat." I motioned at the bench and waited for him to slide into it. "Coffee?"

"Yes, please."

"Rudy, refill for me and another for my friend here."

Rudy smirked at me from behind the counter, and I knew what he was thinking. That was the farthest thing from the truth. I was impatient to find out what happened the other night, but I waited for Rudy to approach with the coffeepot and an extra mug.

"Does your date need a menu, or are you planning on being cheap, Clancy?"

"Rudy, don't fuck with me today."

The words must have come out harsher than I'd thought because I caught the kid flinching in my peripheral. Skittish. I was going to have to temper my normally gruff nature.

"Cranky," Rudy muttered, and I waited for him to drop off the menu, then return to the opposite side of the counter.

I watched in horror at the amount of sugar the kid doctored his coffee with and tried to hide my disgust behind my own mug of straight, black coffee. The way coffee was meant to be drank. Andy's hands shook, and if I hadn't paid closer attention, I would've missed that. I warred with the decision to let Andy take the lead and start the conversation or broach the subject myself.

My curiosity won. "Why did you contact me?"

"I researched the case. A crime reporter, I can't remember his name right now, well, he did some stories and your name was mentioned. Your name came up in several articles."

"But why are you here? I'm not a cop."

Those four simple words still stung my pride. I should be on the case. Who's to say that I wouldn't have caught the guy sometime in the last six months.

I observed the kid, his shoulders slumped and looking very much defeated. Andy raised his mug to his mouth with both hands and slowly sipped at it. The mug connected a little too heavily with the table when he set it down.

"You're doing fine. No need to be nervous."

Andy nodded. I figured he needed a few minutes, so I called Rudy over to take the kid's order. I raised my hand to cover my smile at the amount of food Andy ordered. And he was so animated while he talked to Rudy, I had to admit it was cute.

"You got enough room for all this, kid?" Rudy asked.

I didn't miss the color that highlighted Andy's perfect cheekbones. I had the unbidden thought that the kid could be a model.

"Rudy, just get the kid his food."

Rudy grumped and once again left us alone.

"I'm not a kid," Andy whispered.

"Compared to me, you definitely are. So, keep going."

"I thought with me witnessing part of the..." Andy's voice cracked.

It seemed that Andy was only seconds away from breaking down.

"Take your time, we're not in a hurry." I twisted a bit to dig my notebook out of my jacket. I tried to remain calm and empathetic.

"I thought since I sort of saw the guy that the police would put me in protective custody or something. Maybe that's all on TV. They just have a car where I'm staying, but not all the time."

"What happened before you witnessed the crime?"

I hesitated on saying murder because I had a feeling the kid would completely break down, and I needed some answers first.

"I came home after work. The door was unlocked and that was strange, but I just thought Francis brought someone home. Got distracted, maybe."

"Was it normal for Francis to bring someone home?"

"He wasn't a slut or anything."

I liked Andy's defense of his friend. Loyalty was a big thing for me. I grew up on the streets, not homeless, but I ran my turf more than I was at home. If I couldn't trust the person watching my back, I sensed it almost immediately. That was why I trusted Andy. My gut had kept me alive this long.

"I didn't imply that he was. Did Francis have a regular place he went?"

"Not really. When he went out, he club hopped with a group, but they always ended at Epiphany. It's a gay club."

"I've worked a few cases there." I didn't tell him that those cases had to do with the previous murders. "Have you ever been there?"

"No, well, a time or two, but my job is very demanding. Augustine's, I work as a server."

I whistled, that was upscale and way out of my price range.

"Ritzy place."

"I worked my way up from busser to server. Augustine put

me on one night, and I've been a server ever since. I like it, but when I'm not working I like to be at home."

Pride at his accomplishment was clear in Andy's voice.

"I hate to ask, but what happened after you entered your apartment?"

"I went in and nothing seemed out of place. I called out to get Francis' attention, but nothing, and I heard a thud I think. I got worried that Francis might have had too much to drink. Fell or something. When I went to his room I yelled something about him being dressed. I opened the door and I froze. I couldn't do anything. He was on the floor. Blood was everywhere."

I stretched my arm across the table and took Andy's hand. His skin was soft. Fine pale hairs covered the back of it. The tears were beading on the kid's lower lashes and with my free hand, I handed Andy a napkin.

"Thank you."

"You're welcome."

Andy wiped his eyes as he tried to look everywhere but at me.

"His face and chest were all cut up; it looked like his killer was trying to remove his—"

"It's fine. Take a few breaths. Like I said, we're in no rush right now. Maybe we can just talk while you eat your food."

I gave Andy's hand one last squeeze and then released it. I straightened and went back to drinking my coffee.

"Here you go." Rudy set down the coffeepot on the edge of the table, placed two plates and a bread plate in front of Andy.

I didn't think I ate that much in a day, but I also wasn't living the healthiest life with my work schedule. Rudy refilled our mugs. I was glad he wasn't lingering and acting nosy. I think Andy, as much as he appeared to be keeping his shit together, was scared. To be honest, I was thinking my questioning for the day was over. Pushing Andy too quickly would make him shut down.

"You're not eating," Andy said.

"I'm good. The coffee is good and I think I eat most meals here."

"Francis used to come here."

"Rudy's has been a fixture in this neighborhood since the fifties. I remember being a punk-ass kid thinking I was some gangster and coming in here."

"You're from here?"

I didn't like talking about myself, but to put Andy a bit more at ease I'd allow him his questions.

"A couple blocks up the street. Back in the day I ran numbers for a local bookie." I picked the tamest of my indiscretions to make sure he stayed relaxed.

"You were a cop."

"I wasn't always a cop. My pre-cop past is slightly shady." I felt myself smile at Andy's grin.

I patiently answered questions as Andy finished off his food and drank two more mugs of coffee, realizing for what this meeting was, I felt relaxed. My shoulders weren't tense and I wasn't balancing on the edge of a migraine. It was nice and I didn't exactly know how to handle that. I had to remind myself this was about the case. I wasn't on a date or hanging out with a friend.

"Can you help me?"

Andy's tone was so young and unsure, and even with all the practice I had of putting witnesses at ease I didn't know if I could be at all helpful this time.

"How do you think I can help you?"

"I don't know, find the guy. I'm tired of being on edge. Wondering when I leave my place if he's going to find me. Kill me. The cops aren't taking it seriously, and I don't know what to do."

"Are you staying with someone?"

"Yes, a friend from work. She said I could stay as long as I want, but I have to go home at some point. I need some stuff."

"Why don't I go with you? Call and ask if forensics has released the scene, if they have I can take you over, and you can pack up a few things."

"I don't know if I can go back there."

"Then make me a list and I'll get your things. It would give me a chance to take a look around the scene."

"You'd do that?"

"You have my number. Think it over and just text or call me. We can arrange something. But can I ask you a favor?"

"Sure."

I turned to the next empty page of my notebook, placed my fingertips in the center of it and slid it along with a pen toward Andy. "Write down the names of Francis' friends, family, and if you can remember where they work or live."

Andy nodded and his shaggy hair fell across his forehead. He bent his head and started writing.

"I'll do some checking while you think about what you want to do with getting your clothes and stuff. Andy," I said his name and waited for his gaze to meet mine.

The pale blue of his eyes shocking against the darkness of his lashes. I shouldn't be noticing that shit, but they kept hitting me at the oddest times.

"If at any time you feel unsafe or as if someone is watching you, call me. Don't hesitate, understand?"

"Yes, Mr. Clancy."

"I already told you to call me Ray."

We spoke a while longer as I filled in a few details in my notes, and I asked if Andy needed a ride home. He shook his head and said he needed to clear his head. I wanted to protest.

The kid did come to me because he felt unsafe, but I didn't have any right to order him around.

I paid for Andy's food and our coffee, then I walked him across the street to the bus stop. I pointed out where my office was and reminded him to never hesitate to call. I stood there on the curb a long time after Andy had boarded the bus and disappeared.

I didn't know if it was my fall from grace or how when I was working the case I hadn't been anywhere near solving it that made me so obsessed with finishing it. The killer never left anything behind. A witness like Andy was a mistake the guy had never made before. I had to wonder if the fuck up was on purpose. Was Andy an unwilling part of a trap?

I forced myself to make my way to my office and added the new details to my board. I spun it to face my couch and took a seat. The furniture was lumpy, just a secondhand couch I'd picked up for a few bucks, but at that moment it was the most comfortable thing I'd ever sat on. I just needed a nap, and as I started to doze off my brain filled with crimes scene images and teary pale blue eyes filled with terror.

7

ANDY

Since this all happened with Francis, terror and despair became permanent emotional residents. Sitting at Rudy's with Ray was the first time I felt safe. I knew Elise tried her best to make me comfortable and not afraid, but if the killer stormed her apartment there wasn't anything she could do to save me. I didn't get that feeling from Ray. I knew if I was in danger he'd jump in front to save me. The thought of that exhausted me. Because with Ray fear didn't own me and keep me alert. I started to let my guard down, and in those moments, all the sleep I wasn't getting began to poke at me.

Ray being as dreamy as he was likely was the only reason I didn't go face first into my lunch.

I wasn't sure if that was my wet fantasy talking or the fact I knew he was a cop. Protect and serve and all that. Hearing he ran numbers and had a darker past should have made me warier of his help. But it just solidified he'd know what dark corners to look in. It made a weird kind of sense to me.

Ray's offer to go to my place to get things I needed both relaxed me and made me nervous. I didn't own fancy things, and I wore my boxers until the elastic and fabric was threadbare. I could afford to grab some new boxers, so I'd just ask for some clothes, my ancient laptop, and some minor essentials. I didn't really care what clothes he chose, but I didn't want to make him stressed wondering what to pick.

When the bus stopped by Elise's I hopped off, vigilantly searched my surroundings and began walking toward her place. There was a department store a few blocks past her complex, so I decided to grab some boxers before returning to her apartment.

As much as I loved cool superhero boxers I often just went with the cheapest pair. I chose to consider myself frugal. Not like anyone was going to see what I had under my jeans, boring standard colors it was. I grabbed a few bags, and as I was waiting in line, I saw Gabin enter the store. It was odd seeing him in public. He always wore expensive clothes, his shoes always shined, and he literally walked with his nose up.

He didn't see me and I observed him like an animal in the zoo. There were dark rings under his eyes, and I knew it was likely because of the situation with him and Augustine wearing him down.

With my back to the store, I heard him ask behind me for assistance. I placed my boxers on the belt, trying to be discreet, I didn't want him to see me. I was just paying when from the corner of my eye I saw him at the register in front of me. He was putting condoms on the belt, and while that wouldn't make anyone else react, I did. He and Augustine were married; I assumed they were all protection free. *Maybe he didn't trust him after the affair, or maybe he was having one of his own?* I was going to have to talk to Elise about this.

When I stepped out of the store and turned to walk to Elise's, I heard my name and saw Gabin waving.

"Andrew, my dear." He stood on his toes to kiss both my

cheeks. His normal greeting. "I am dreadfully sorry to hear about the passing of your friend."

I love how brutal murder never left anyone's lips. It was like Francis had a sudden heart attack and that was it.

"Thanks, Gabin."

He eyed me for a moment. "You're staying at Elise's I heard?"

"I am. The police needed me to vacate the premises and whatnot. Thank you, and thank Augustine, for giving me some time. I promise I'll be back in a couple days."

Gabin's nose crinkled in disgust at the mention of his husband, but that was the only impression I got that he was still upset.

"Of course, dear. You simply get back on your feet. If I can do anything, please let me know."

At that he turned and began walking the opposite way I was going. I knew for a fact he didn't live around here so why was he here? Only thing up that street was an apartment complex and a church, and I didn't think Gabin was the praying sort.

The sound of a horn honking at some stupid pedestrian snapped me out of my thoughts, and the fact I was standing there out in the open hit me. Right, someone wants me dead.

As quickly as possible I walked back to Elise's. I liked her building and I made a mental note to ask her if she knew about availabilities and how much rent was. It was a light yellow, not obnoxious but like the sun itself kissed it. Everything was accented in white and all the windows had flower boxes. Some tenants had flowers in them but most didn't. Spring was long gone and the chill in the air wasn't making people plant anything. I loved that you needed a code to get into the building and that the people seemed friendly. If a killer was chasing you and you hollered for them to call 911, they would actually help you.

No doubt about it, I was never living in my old apartment

again even after it was cleared. Not a chance so I best start figuring out what I was going to do.

Knowing Elise was closing tonight I made myself a sandwich for dinner, camped out on her couch, and got lost in Cake Wars on TV.

I must have dozed off because the sound of someone entering Elise's apartment made me jolt awake. I stood fast, grabbed the remote, and readied myself to defend my life.

"Chill out, Andy, it's just me," Elise said with a chuckle. "Were you going to hit me with that or maybe..." She gasped in mock horror. "Mute me?"

"Shut up." I tossed the remote on the couch and followed her into the kitchen. I sat at her table as she fixed herself a glass of wine to unwind.

"There were cops down the street. The Parker Complex. Wonder what happened over there. I had to take a different route home." She sat at the table watching me as she drank.

"Parker?" She nodded and I remembered Gabin walking that way earlier. "Let's turn on the news."

Once we sat on the couch, we flipped to the evening news. Sure enough, after a few minutes a newscaster appeared live from near Parker.

"There's very little to go on at this point, Richard. Police aren't talking and residents seem almost confused. About ten minutes ago a body was removed, but that's all we know right now. One resident said she heard screaming and some thumping around at about nine this evening. She called the police shortly after. She did say how upset she was that the police took almost forty minutes to arrive, and by that time, the sounds stopped. When the police entered, there was one less person in the world. The identity of the victim or the circumstances aren't being released, but as soon as I know more, I'll report it."

Elise quickly shut the television off and ran to the window. Parker was only a mile from her place, so the blue and red lights were visible.

"Do you think—" I started to speak, but Elise cut me off.

"Don't, Andy, let's just wait and see."

Elise and I watched for hours while police cars, news vans, and a parade of other cars and trucks came and went from Parker Apartment Complex. We agreed to walk over there in the morning and see if some of the people who lived there could tell us what happened.

The police not giving a shit didn't surprise me. Their priority was for the upper-class, not us here. Even though Elise lived on the better, poor side of New West City, it was still a no rush zone for authorities.

We both fell asleep on her couch to the sound of infomercials. When the sun finally rose, the news was reporting a murder over at Parker. When the comparison to the murder matched Francis', I left a message for Ray. I didn't know if he'd heard about it, but this killer was still out there, and as a former cop I had no doubt he'd be able to get information on it that would help find this guy and keep me alive.

Was the killer looking for me? Who was the dead person? What the fuck was happening and why didn't the cops care? Did Gabin have anything to do with it?

My mind raced from rational thinking to ridiculous.

After breakfast, Elise and I cleaned up and got dressed and decided to walk up to the complex. There were a few people sitting outside smoking and talking, so we walked over and asked what the hell happened last night. No point trying to butter anyone up. It wasn't like that where we lived.

"Ethel over on the fourth floor said—Chad, Chester, something like that—some young guy was killed. She said it sounded like he was being attacked," Hank, a guy who lived there, said.

"She said while she was waitin' on the cops it got silent all of a sudden. She knew someone was still there and locked her doors and put a chair blockin' it. Said she heard someone leave right before the cops showed up."

It was all so suspicious and similar. I texted Ray with all the info I got, gave him a small list of things I needed, and told him I'd be at Elise's for the rest of the day.

Like Ethel, I was barricading the door.

Elise had to work the afternoon to close, so when we got back she dressed for work. On her way out, she said to text her every hour to make sure I was okay.

Ray sent me a text shortly after Elise left saying he saw the news, was doing some digging, and would be by Elise's later.

I sat on her couch, clutching a baseball bat she gave me, and waited for Ray like he was the only thing capable of keeping me breathing.

8

RAY

I sat in my car outside Andy's place and tried to go over the details Donnelly had just given me on the new victim. This time nothing had interrupted the killer, and now I was sure this was number five. The newest one, Chad Pembrooke, was a young man in his early twenties, physically similar to the other victims. Again, I didn't have much detail and it was frustrating me. I was dying to get my hands on the case file, but I didn't know how I'd accomplish that.

As I'd listened to Donnelly read the report to me I had a moment of déjà vu. The killer was back and Pembrooke's proximity to Andy was too close for my comfort. I made a mental note to ask around on my way to where Andy was staying.

I'd gone through the list of friends, family, and coworkers Andy had given me. It was only a criminal background search, and other than some misdemeanors, nothing had stood out.

I got out of my car and made my way inside the building of Francis and Andy's apartment, then up to the second floor. The crime scene tape hung down on either side of the door and the seal was broken. I removed my Glock from where it rested heavy and comforting along my ribs. I raised my arm to aim, took a deep, steadying breath and turned the knob, easing the door open.

I made entry, swept the interior, and cleared rooms one by one. When I was satisfied I was alone, I put my weapon away. I strode to the center of the apartment and mentally reconstructed what happened from the information from previous murders and Andy's retelling of when he'd arrived home.

The suspect entered through the door. Why did he pick someone with a roommate? This was the first victim that didn't live alone. Was that the point? The suspect wanted to up the stakes and take out two victims in one night; was that the plan? Each previous murder was planned in minute detail. Was the killer's desperation turning him sloppy?

I strode to Francis' room. The blood splatter and spray spoke of a violent confrontation. Again, a mistake made on the killer's part. Each victim before was taken without struggle, as if the killer had attacked while the target slept, but Francis appeared to have fought back. The bed clothes were thrown back as if Francis' had removed them as he surged from the bed. Could that mean the killer became injured during the attack? A few calls to the local hospitals to inquire about any patients who may have been injured in a fight made it to my list. Although, that would turn into a rabbit hole I'd never escape from just for the fact that the suspect list could expand by hundreds.

Come back to me, the message was left carved into Francis and, now, Pembrooke's chest. It was confusing, and I hated not having the answers.

"What the hell are you doing here, Clancy?"

I spun and automatically reached for my weapon but groaned as I realized Green stood in the opened doorway of the apartment. I was seriously losing my touch if I didn't hear the door open or worse, didn't even think about closing it behind me.

"Just picking some stuff up for a friend of mine. Andy needs some clothes."

I didn't trust anyone and letting my former commanding officer know about even my limited involvement hadn't made it to my to-do list.

Andy seemed like a good kid. Just in the wrong place at the wrong time. But there was something about him I couldn't ignore, and it wasn't only him in need of my help or protection.

"Didn't think the barely legal was your type."

"Fuck you, Green. What are you doing here?"

"I'm a cop, the question is what are you really doing here? You don't have a badge anymore."

"I think I already answered that. Andy needed some clothes." I had a feeling Green was trying to trip me up, but he was an idiot if he thought I'd make that kind of mistake.

"Why don't I supervise while you—"

I walked out of Francis' room and toward Andy's, Green followed me as I knew he would. While trying to ignore Green, I found the duffel bag in Andy's closet and tossed it back onto the unmade bed. Three suit bags, one of them empty, hung in the closet, and I recognized the name of the tailor. I whistled through my teeth. I didn't want to guess how much those three single suits cost.

Andy would have to go back to work at some point, so, I carefully removed them from the closet, and then laid them across the bed and folded the empty to place in the overnight bag.

"Whatever fucked up idea you got in your head, Clancy, this ain't a repeat."

"That's what you want to believe. You can't tell me you aren't suspicious. I fucking swear you and the higher ups will cover this up until the body count gets so high y'all can't ignore that this guy is a serial. More kids are going to die because you can't get your head out of your ass and warn them."

"We've never had a serial in New West City."

The stupidity of the city's police force astounded me more every day. This city at its core was a cesspool. Corruption reigned supreme and no one wanted to address the issue. They'd rather pretend and let innocents get caught in the crossfire. I'd spent my entire life in New West, this wasn't the utopia the city government tried to imagine it was. Dirty cops were an epidemic.

"You can believe that if you want, but facts are different from fiction, and you and the brass have been putting a spin on the truth for decades."

I quickly packed up clothes and rechecked Andy's messages to make sure I wasn't missing anything. To be on the safe side I grabbed an e-reader and chargers from beside Andy's bed.

"Clancy, stay off my case."

"Duly noted."

I slung the straps of the bag over my shoulder and picked up the suit bags. As I went to pass Green, he grabbed my arm.

"You don't back off, I'll make sure you rot in jail."

"You don't want to threaten me. That wife of yours would love to know about that sweet piece you keep tucked away. Isn't he the same age as Sam? Twenty, right? Graduated with your son, didn't he?"

I took satisfaction in the color fading from Green's face. It wasn't a well-kept secret, but Green's wife was a sweet woman. She had no idea about the bastard she truly had for a husband. I wasn't one to judge for getting a bit of strange on the side. That was a couple's business. Yet that didn't mean I wouldn't take Green down in a heartbeat.

"Don't fuck with me, Green. You don't have any power over me anymore. And if I ever get proof that you're giving up the young gay kids in New West as sacrificial lambs, I'll take you out in a fucking second."

I pulled away from his suddenly slack grip and strode to the door. I took the steps to the first floor and exited the building. Before getting into the driver's side, I stowed Andy's belongings on the passenger seat. I checked the street and pulled out into the slow-moving afternoon traffic.

My brain wouldn't shut down with all the what-ifs and the growing lists of mistakes the killer had made. It wasn't their M.O. and I started to wonder if they'd happened on purpose as a way to call someone out—to call me out. I glanced into my rearview mirror and recognized Green's car. That wouldn't do, so, as I made my way toward Andy I took a left, then a right, and another left, and the car remained on my tail.

The traffic light ahead was about to turn red and I gunned the engine. I drove into the intersection and took a sharp right. Car horns and curses came through the open windows of my car, but it had served its purpose. Green was stuck at the light. What's the worst that could happen? A traffic ticket. My glove box was filled with those.

I didn't want to take any more chances and started driving straight to where Andy was staying. I'd park, drop off Andy's things, and then walk to the newest crime scene. Another twenty minutes passed before I reached the address Andy gave me.

After some creative use of profanity, I found a parking space down the block. I hurried back to the entrance. I double checked the apartment number and made my way up. A couple arguing, their raised voices easily traveled through a door. A baby crying. Children's laughter.

I stopped in front of an apartment door and raised my hand, I knocked.

"Andy, it's Clancy."

I announced myself to put the young man at ease. I smiled as the door cracked open and Andy peeked through the crack. His dark hair covered one eye. I still couldn't get over how pretty

Andy was and inwardly jerked at the inappropriateness of my thoughts. I shouldn't notice anything about the kid because I was only there to try to keep him safe.

"Hi, Ray." Andy backed up, opening the door as he went.

"I think I got everything you asked for," I said as I entered the apartment and handed over the bags.

"Thank you."

Super soft fingertips grazed over my hand, and I tried to mask the moment I jerked back. The corners of Andy's wide, full lips were pulled into a shy smile. I brought my attention to the space. It was a feminine place with all those homey touches that made a home a home. My house looked shabby in comparison. The last time I'd gone there I'd made mental notes to take care of dusting and laundry.

"Nice place."

"Elise has been really nice about letting me stay. You brought my suits?"

"I figured you'd have to go back to work at some point and wanted to make sure you didn't have to go back to the apartment. Have you thought about what you're going to do about a place to live?"

"Elise said that I could stay with her as long as I wanted, but I'd love to have my own space. Would you like a cup of coffee? I just made a pot."

"That would be great."

I observed as Andy carefully hung the suits in a tiny closet off the living room, and then I followed him to the kitchen.

"Did you find anything?"

The question had a definite vocal shake in it, and I made myself take a seat at the small table instead of trying to comfort the young man. That wasn't my responsibility. Yeah, I had a soft spot for the kid. He was in a shitty situation and he was scared, I didn't even want to have something inappropriate happen. I had to remind myself that I needed to keep a professional distance.

I removed my jacket and twisted to hang it on the back of my chair. I caught him staring at my gun.

"Safety is on, it's a tool of the trade."

"Do you have to use it a lot?"

"No, not really; P.I.'s don't really have the exciting lives that are portrayed on television. Sometimes I wish, just to break up the boredom a bit."

Andy darted a glance at me and gave another one of those sweet smiles. I needed to change the subject, get my thoughts away from Andy and onto the case.

"Did Francis take any form of self-defense class?" Andy placed two mugs on the table, and I thanked him as I wrapped my hands around one of them.

"Well, he had this crush on this guy at a gym and decided to take a class, but I don't think it really went anywhere beyond a few classes."

Andy took a seat and I took in his clothes. It was the same outfit he'd worn when we'd met at Rudy's. The clothing was clean but they'd seen better days, just like the clothes I'd packed up for him.

"Was Francis a fighter? I found evidence of a struggle. When I was on the case, the killer typically attacked while the victims were sleeping."

"He wasn't a fighter, but he wouldn't back down. He got bullied a lot in high school and swore it wouldn't happen again."

"Can you think back for me, did you notice anyone following you, or maybe Francis mentioned someone?"

Andy slowly sipped at his coffee, and I waited for him to think it over.

"Not really, no one following me, and the only thing Francis mentioned was some creepy guy trying to pick him up at Epiphany a month or so ago, but really, that's not unheard of."

"Now, was there anything recently that bothered you?"

"Well, I was at the store and I saw Gabin, he works at Augustine's and is Augustine's husband. He doesn't live around here, but he was buying condoms. It was before the newest murder."

I dug out my notebook and made a note to speak with Gabin.

"Does Gabin have a boyfriend that could work or live in the area?"

"I wouldn't think so, but Gabin found out Augustine was cheating, so, it could've been a revenge hookup."

"Possibly," I muttered as I made more notes.

"What are you writing down? You do that a lot."

"Just notes, one to check out Gabin and maybe ask him a few questions."

"People normally use smartphones or tablets to take notes."

"I'm a bit old school. I have boxes of these notebooks I've used over the years. Do you mind if I ask you some personal questions?"

"That should be okay." Andy seemed to get nervous and was using his thumbnail to pick at the printed logo of some diner on his mug.

"Do you have an ex-boyfriend that might hold a grudge or a date that went wrong?"

"I don't date, work is demanding, and I don't think I've had a boyfriend that would worry about killing someone or me. Do you think someone was after me?"

"No, no, there's no evidence of that, but we need to cover all the bases."

I spent the evening asking questions and Andy answering them. It got later, and I offered to buy dinner. We talked about things other than the killings, and I enjoyed the company the young man offered. Andy had a beautiful laugh and again, I was taken aback by my thoughts. I was failing at the professional distance, and I didn't know how to stop it. If I didn't keep my head in the game I was going to fuck up this case, and I wanted to catch this guy, get him off the streets, but more than that, I wanted to make sure Andy was safe. And those thoughts were starting to trouble me the most.

9

ANDY

Ray stayed until Elise returned from work. They talked for a while, Elise grilled him on whether or not we were safe. Around the time she asked Ray if she should get a gun permit, I realized she was beyond terrified, and I was the reason for her fear. Elise and I may have only been work buddies for a long time, but the second she let me into her home to keep me safe, she became more.

With Chad's murder and it being so close to where she lived, it was obviously weighing on her that the killer would find me and she'd be a casualty. I understood that paranoia; I was living it daily.

"Ray?" I called after him as he walked down the corridor of Elise's building. He stopped and a raised eyebrow, the only invitation I got to speak. "It's not safe for Elise if I'm here."

He surveyed the hall before answering. "If the killer is after you, and that's a possibility, anyone in your path will be in danger. I won't sugar coat it up for you, Andy."

I feared that. "I don't want to lose anyone else, I can't," I whispered almost to myself, but Ray heard. He stood a few inches in front of me, his hand gently touched my arm, and there was sympathy in his gaze.

"Give me a few days, I'll see about securing you a safe place, one close to work even." Ray's eyes flitted over my face. "This isn't your fault and I'll do everything I can to catch this son of a bitch and keep you safe."

I don't know why I did it or what came over me, but without overthinking it I crashed my lips against Ray's. For a moment I thought he'd push me away and tell me I was gross and stupid. But he didn't.

His hand that rested on my arm slid over my shoulder and stopped when he cupped my cheek. His lips were warm, rough, and when he returned my kiss it felt like I was breathing for the first time in days.

It only lasted a moment and when I pulled away there wasn't a look of disgust on Ray's face like I thought there'd be, there was hunger in those eyes. Hunger for me and in that moment, I wished we were behind closed doors so I could see how far I could push the detective.

"I have to go," Ray said roughly. "I'll call tomorrow, hopefully with a place that will be safe." He cleared his throat and I watched as he walked quickly down the hallway.

When he was out of sight I felt the loss, and in an instant, the fear was suffocating.

Sleep didn't come easy for me, but when it did I dreamt of Ray and all the things I wanted to do to him.

ONE HOUR. I WAS GONE FOR ONE HOUR AFTER ELISE LEFT FOR work. All I needed was more deodorant, so I walked down to the department store I was at the day before. When I returned there were three police cars, and they wouldn't let me enter the building.

"What's going on?" I asked a cop standing by the front.

"Please step back." He went to touch me, but I jumped back.

"I'm staying here, I think I'm allowed to know why I can't get inside." The fact that Elise wasn't there dampened my worry, but I was nervous nonetheless. I had a suspicion.

"There was a break-in at one of the apartments, someone called it in, and that's all I can tell you."

That was strange. Why would they close off the whole building for a break-in?

I stood by the curb with a few of Elise's neighbors. Every one of them confused as to why they were all asked to exit the building or not be allowed to enter. I took the time to text Ray and let him know the little information I had.

"Andy?" I heard Elise's voice and turned. She was in her server uniform, eyes frantically searching. "Andy, where are you?"

"Elise," I shouted just as a man exited the building. I recognized him from the three question interview he gave me the night of Francis' murder. The Chief, I thought. Green. He was a typical looking chief. White, thinning hair, pale skin that was in serious need of a facial or something. His suit, while clearly expensive, didn't fit the cheap man wearing it, it was very unflattering, or maybe it was the rather round beer belly he was sporting that made it all wrong. There was nothing welcoming about him. He left me with an uneasy feeling that turning away from him in favor of my friend was a welcome thing.

"Oh, Andy, thank god. I got a call from the police saying someone broke into my apartment. I thought..." She burst into tears and with every ounce of courage I had, I wrapped her in my arms and whispered lies in her ear. I did this to her.

"It's okay, I'm fine, Elise. I wasn't here, I needed pit stick."

Her chuckle was watery, but she stopped crying.

"Ms. Summers, Elise Summers?" Green asked, now standing a foot from us.

"Yes." She faced him and held her hand out as he introduced himself.

"I'm afraid you're not going to be able to enter your apartment. Is there some place you can stay for the evening? I'm sure we will get it all wrapped up by morning."

I could tell she was thinking, and when her eyes locked with mine I knew she was worrying about what I'd do.

"Don't worry about me, El. I'll call Ray, ask if he can help for a night." She shook her head.

"Yeah, I can stay with my sister. She's an hour away, but it'll be fine."

Green wasn't paying any attention to Elise anymore, his main focus was on me.

"Ray?" he asked, his pale face getting redder by the second. "Ray Clancy by any chance?"

I nodded, unsure why that was making the large man look like he was about to go off like a tea kettle.

"I know you, Allen something, you were a witness I spoke with briefly the other day." He folded his arms over his chest and glared at me.

"It's Andy, Andrew Shay. I was staying with Elise."

His light blue eyes flickered to Elise and back to me. "You family?"

"A friend. As a matter of fact, remember my roommate Francis was killed a few nights ago. The police told me to leave my place, so I was staying with Elise. Now you're saying I can't stay there anymore." I could feel my own blood start to boil. "You all didn't give a shit about my safety then, and I'm guessing this break-in has something to do with what happened to Francis. Are you all going to care about me now or am I still on my own?"

At this point Elise had her arms wrapped around my waist, but she seemed just as furious as I was.

"Mr. Shay. We have no proof that this is connected to—"

"Bullshit." The sound of Ray's voice was like an entire army appearing to defend me. "Don't treat him like he's an idiot. You and I both know it's connected. Keeping information from him will get him killed."

"I told you to stay off my case," Green shouted, pointing a finger dangerously close to Ray's face.

"Maybe if you actually did your fucking job I wouldn't have to be here right now." Ray didn't back down an inch from the larger man.

"Please," Elise's voice was soft, pleading, "can you tell us something about the break-in?"

Green narrowed his eyes once more at Ray, lowered his hand, and looked down at Elise.

"Like I was saying, there's no way of knowing if this is connected. I don't go around assuming things." He eyed Ray. "But I can tell you whoever did that was sending a message. Maybe to Ms. Summers, maybe to you, Mr. Shay."

"What message?" Ray asked.

Green ignored Ray's existence and spoke to Elise and me. "They vandalized the apartment and wrote on your wall. It said 'He's Mine.' We have no idea what it means. Do you have a disgruntled ex, Ms. Summers?"

'He's Mine'? Who?

"No. I haven't dated in over a year and we parted on good terms." She seemed confused, but I wasn't and one look at Ray's face told me he wasn't either.

"If you could follow me to the station, Ms. Summers, I'd like to get the ex's information. Just to rule him out." They started to walk away when she stopped and was about to speak to me.

"I'm fine, El. I'm going to grab some stuff and I'll be with Ray." She nodded and went with Green.

"With me?" Ray asked.

Yeah, I had a feeling that was going to get his attention.

"We both know that message was for me. I don't know what it means, but I know I can't endanger my friends and I don't want to die. That means you're going to have to keep me safe."

Ray smirked, and it was beyond sexy. I wanted to lick it away and plunder his mouth.

"I'll see about grabbing your stuff." He tossed me his keys. "Wait for me in my car."

I was glad he didn't fight me on it. I was tired of bouncing around, but I was more tired of being terrified all the time. Ray made me feel safe, and the fact he was a walking wet dream helped a lot, too.

10

RAY

As soon as I'd gotten the text from Andy letting me know someone had broken into Elise's apartment I was in my car and headed across the city. I'd seen this coming, but now everything was even more complicated by the kiss. It wasn't like the thought hadn't entered my mind. Yet I'd promised myself I would keep my distance. But Andy's lips were soft and gave just right under mine. When he'd pulled away, I'd almost grabbed him to pull him back against me—just for one more kiss. If I was truthful with myself, I wanted more than a kiss, and I needed to figure out how to—what, forget about it, because that wasn't happening.

I'd been enough of a nuisance to get into the apartment just to grab what I'd dropped off to Andy yesterday. It appeared my reputation got me at least a toe in the door. I didn't know how much leverage I'd have when I started to dig deeper into the case.

The interior of Elise's trashed apartment spoke of rage and in my gut, I knew this had to do with more than just the killer wanting to make a threat. No, this was someone becoming unhinged. When Andy said he was staying with me, I didn't have any other choice than my place.

The ride to my house seemed to take forever since it was made in silence. The shabby exterior came into view. It wasn't in the best neighborhood, but this was the place I grew up and when my mother died it came to me. Luckily, it was paid off. I'd hate to lose it. Unfortunately, my job wasn't paying the bills for both the office and home.

I drove into the garage and hit the opener causing the door to come down, sending the interior into darkness except for the light streaming through a single window over my dad's old workbench.

"Here we are; come on, I'll get you settled."

Andy just nodded and I wondered if it was finally catching up with him. I grabbed the bags from the backseat, and we exited the garage into an overgrown backyard. It reminded me, yet again, I hadn't kept up like I should have; my mom would be ashamed at what I'd let go.

I unlocked the back door and stepped aside to let Andy go first. When I walked in behind him, I dropped the duffel bag on the floor and draped the suit bags over the back of a chair.

"You live here by yourself?"

I chuckled at Andy's question, I swore there was more to it than wondering if I had a roommate. I removed my jacket and threw it onto the island.

"Yeah, my dad died when I was in my teens, and my mother about five years ago. When she passed away, the house became mine."

"I'm sorry."

"No need to apologize. My mother was miserable for a long time without my dad. She tried, but she was never the same."

My parents were the epitome of happily married. They were that couple that all others looked up to, and I was a shit growing up. I'd made my mom's life more difficult after dad had died.

"Do you spend a lot of time here?"

Andy walked past the kitchen table and drew a line in the dust.

"No, as you can see, it's a bit of a mess. Let me show you to your room, and then we can go to the store to see about getting a few things. The fridge is empty."

"I don't want to be a bother."

"You're not. If you're staying here, there needs to be food and coffee. Coffee is a requirement for functioning."

"Definitely."

I liked that he was more relaxed and as I passed him, I stroked my hand along Andy's lower back. When he attempted to move closer, I released him and strode toward the stairs. Andy's little frustrated huff was cute. I had to admit it stroked my ego a bit. Problem was I was unsure if the attraction was some transference type thing. He was reliant on me keeping him safe and maybe it was gratitude for my help. I really needed to get my shit together. It wasn't like I was averse to a little fun, but Andy kind of had this aura of someone who liked commitment, and what promises could I make in this situation?

I led him upstairs and to the room across from mine.

"Here you go, bathroom is at the end of the hall." As I spoke I opened the curtains to let in the light, and then turned on the lamp. "My room is across the hall."

"Ray?"

"Yeah."

"I...I really just appreciate this. I know I didn't give you much choice."

"Andy." I approached him and raised my arms to wrap my hands around his slim biceps. "It was probably going to happen at some point. I should've anticipated the warning."

Andy stood a few inches shorter than me, and I couldn't miss the way his gaze kept dropping to my mouth. I didn't think about it, I took one step and another until I backed him up against the wall beside the door. He licked his lips and I forgot all the excuses why I couldn't let it happen.

I stroked my left hand up his arm and over his shoulder. I loved the way his pupils dilated as I fisted my hand in his soft hair. With a gentle jerk I brought his lips to mine. The groan that rumbled my chest at the contact took me by surprise. I used my heavier mass to trap him against the wall. Andy's hands flattened on my lower back.

I bit at the full curves of his lips. I didn't rush, people might think I was big and gruff with not enough manners, but moments like these I needed to savor. I kissed him until he was moaning and arching into me; I teased his tongue with mine. My cock jerked where it was pushed to his, and it brought me back to my senses.

Reluctantly I broke the kiss and rested our foreheads together. Our breathing was ragged and we kept moving our mouths closer as if we couldn't resist just one more connection, no matter how brief.

"We should go."

"Did I do something wrong?" Andy's voice wavered, and his cheeks flushed. I could tell he was embarrassed.

"No, fuck, no, not...not in the least, we just..." I angled my head to the side to steal one more kiss. My control balanced on the edge, and it wouldn't take much to push me over. Andy felt delicate and just right against me. The young man stole my control so easily. "I can't keep you safe if all I can think about is getting you in my bed."

"I'm an adult, I know what I want, Ray."

My hand in his hair angled his head to the side until I could nip at his throat, and I retreated to take in the heaviness of his eyelids. "I know you're an adult. We just can't do this, not right now. Fuck, you make it impossible to think."

I brought my right hand up to cup his jaw, my thumb caressing the pout of his bottom lip. I rubbed our covered dicks together, and he was so pretty when he whined and trembled. With one last kiss I made myself put distance between us. I studied Andy, the way he leaned heavily against the wall, and his chest moved in a frantic rhythm as he tried to catch his breath. The arch of his body pulled his t-shirt up to expose a pale, smooth strip of belly.

The awe that I could do that to a man as young and beautiful as Andy made me speechless. All I wanted to do was grab him and take him to my room, lay him across my bed. My hard-on was getting out of control.

"We're going to leave and go to the store in ten minutes. I'm going to go change and meet you downstairs."

I escaped and when I passed Andy, I resisted the urge to pull him back against me. One more kiss wouldn't be enough, and if I didn't put distance between us, I was going to take this to a place neither of us were ready to go.

When I entered my room, I shrugged off my shoulder holster and laid it on my dresser. I worked the buttons of my dress shirt free and removed it and the t-shirt under it to throw it in the overflowing laundry basket. I didn't waste time, I changed into jeans and a black t-shirt that exposed the numerous tattoos that covered my arms but concealed the others. Some of them weren't ones I was proud of, but had kept them to remind myself of the past. My mistakes shaped who I am, and I still had friends who could help. I felt my mouth pull into a smirk at what Andy would think about his prospective protection detail. We'd save that reveal for the next day.

My arousal was barely under control. It would kill me to stay away. I was going to keep my cock under control no matter how much I wanted Andy. It wouldn't be fair to him.

"Ray."

I turned to find Andy in the doorway. I grabbed my tactical boots and sat on the edge of my bed to put them on.

"What's wrong?"

"Nothing, I was thinking if it was safe enough for me to be here, maybe I'd just stay here while you go shopping."

"Are you sure?" I didn't like the thought of him being alone, but the store was only down the street. A little neighborhood mom and pop store. My alarm system would alert my phone, and the motion detectors would send pictures of anyone who came on the property.

"Yes."

"Okay, stay in the house and away from windows. I'll turn on the alarm system before I leave."

"Ray..."

"Andy, it's going to be fine, I promise. No need to be scared. Just remain cautious of your surroundings. Tomorrow, be prepared to go to work with me. Get some rest and just relax until I get back." I straightened and closed the distance between us. "I promise, Andy, I'll make sure you stay safe. You just have to trust me."

"I do."

I raised my hand to stroke Andy's smooth cheek and he leaned into the touch. He was so receptive to my affections. It went to my head quicker than my favorite Scotch. I had to remind myself this wasn't permanent, that I couldn't keep him, no matter how much my brain and body wanted to hold on and not let go.

11

ANDY

After Ray left I found myself in desperate need to keep myself busy. My mind was my own worst enemy. Why would I think Ray would want to have sex with me? Kissing was one thing, but to see me naked? I couldn't blame him for backing off.

Growing up kids at school called me In-The-Way-Shay because I was always so knobby and knocked things over. My mom told me I often reminded her of a giraffe. While that may not seem like an insult, it was.

Under Ray's kitchen sink I was surprised not only to actually find cleaning supplies, but they were unopened. He was either the laziest, slobbiest person ever or he really was never here.

There weren't any dishes in the sink, so I went about spraying down the counters, sink, all the appliances. When I was happy that the sheen of dust was gone, I went to working on the floors. While I cleaned, my mind raced to scenarios. Ray was nice, he didn't outright say I wasn't his type or that he thought I was weird. But I knew. Guys who fucked me did it in the back of clubs and with the lights off. Men like Ray never even looked at me twice. I wasn't as beautiful as Francis was, but I wasn't so ugly no one touched me. There was just that moment right after orgasm the other guy looked disgusted.

I don't know why I flirted. Ugh! The more upset I got with myself the cleaner Ray's house got. The musty, stagnant odor that once filled the air was replaced with lemon and lavender.

I meant it when I said I trusted Ray, I did. There was an honesty to him, a gritty, raw honesty. He kept people safe. It didn't matter he said his past was shady. Who he was now was a good person. I was so conflicted.

I was in the room Ray assigned me tucking in the clean sheets when I heard the front door.

"Andy?" Ray shouted.

I didn't answer, just went toward him. As I got closer, I heard him mumbling.

"Did he polish the legs of the couch, too? Jesus, I didn't know that was a black entertainment system, I thought it was brown."

"I was just as shocked," I said smiling, when he jumped at the sound of my voice.

He turned and the expression on his face had me laughing. He just stared at me, but after a few seconds he chuckled.

"You didn't have to do this, Andy." He walked past me and placed a couple bags on the clean table. "Wow, in here, too?"

"I really did have to, Ray. It's healthier this way and it smells good." I sniffed dramatically earning another chuckle.

"I just have a couple more bags in the car, I'll be right back."

I began unpacking the bags while Ray brought the others in. He had a lot of pasta, two steaks, hot dogs, burger patties, basically bachelor food. If it wasn't for Augustine's, I would never have learned how to cook. There were a few things missing from some recipes I knew, but maybe I could make this work.

"I'm not a big cook. I mostly eat at a cart on the street or Rudy's." He shrugged and his sheepish look had me thinking how much I wanted to kiss him again. The sobering memory of why I wasn't going to shook me from those lust-filled thoughts.

"Fortunately for you, I work in a five-star restaurant and have learned a few things." I rolled up my sleeves as I reached for the two steaks. "Why don't you go do whatever it is you do and I'll make dinner."

"I don't need you waiting on me, Andy." He seemed equally upset and embarrassed.

"It's a thank you for helping me, Ray. I'll also pay you, but I need to do this, please?"

Ray did in fact go do his whatever things and I began cooking. Remembering everything Max, the head chef from Augustine's, had taught me wasn't hard because he yelled them at me. Like I was on autopilot, I just cooked.

I was just plating everything when my phone rang. It was an unknown number so I thought perhaps it was Elise calling from her sister's.

"Hello?" I answered as I placed the butter sauce in a bowl.

"You can't have what's mine," the robotic voice said over the phone.

"I'm sorry, what?" Prank calls were—wait no. "Why are you bothering me?"

"I will find you." It was the last thing the voice said before they hung up.

"Ray!" I shouted as I ran out of the kitchen. "Ray."

I heard him running just as I turned into the living room.

"Andy? What is it?"

"I got a call." I handed him my phone where the unknown number was still displayed. "It was a robot voice, like one of those devices that masks the person's real voice?" He nodded as he walked over to the small table next to the couch and pulled out a pad. "They said 'you can't have what's mine' and 'I will find you.'"

He was writing the number down along with everything I said.

"How'd they get your number?" I didn't know if Ray was asking me or talking to himself, but I answered anyway.

"Same way they found out I was at Elise's. Same way they seem to know a lot of things. They're following me and they're smart." I huffed and went back to the kitchen.

"Andy?" Ray followed behind me. "Ever hear the saying there's always a bigger fish?" Of course I had, I was five once, I nodded. "Yeah, well, we're the bigger fish and we're gonna find this guy and he will pay."

We didn't speak much after that. While I poured our drinks Ray sat, pad in hand thinking.

"Eat, Ray. I'm sure you'll have a lot of work to do tonight figuring this out so you better eat." My hands shook as I grabbed my fork and knife.

Even though I was at Ray's and safer than I was at Elise's, the fact the killer called me, touched me when I was at my safe place, unnerved me.

"This is delicious, Andy."

I blushed under the praise, I didn't get a lot of it. I was no Gordon Ramsey, but I got by. Eating at the food court constantly would've become costly, and if I was going to spend money, I'd rather splurge on groceries to make Francis and me small dinners and lunches.

"Thanks. It's financially better and healthier. Enjoy."

We ate in silence; the clinking of our utensils filled the air. I glimpsed at Ray a few times and he caught my eye, winked and went back to eating.

He really didn't seem worried about the call. And I asked him why.

"Your phone isn't linked to this address, so whoever this is can't track you here..."

"Unless they're smart enough to know how to track a phone."

Ray shook his head. "True, but then why not just come here, why call at all? I don't think they know you're here yet."

"Maybe they needed me to answer to be able to track it." I watched too many cop dramas, and by the look on Ray's face, he agreed.

"Let's focus on what they said to you. 'You can't have what's mine,' what's that mean? What do you have? And 'I will find you.' That solidifies they don't know where you are." He was writing again, his plate empty and pushed aside.

"How could I have anything this person wants? He killed Francis not me. They didn't even know I was there until I opened the door. None of it makes sense." The frustration that filled my veins finally burst through, and I swiped my plate off the table and sobbed when it crashed to the floor shattering into a million pieces. It was all too much. I missed not being able to call or sit with Francis to talk about everything, and I didn't understand what Ray saw in me if anything, and someone wanted me dead.

"Andy." Ray was so close I could smell his after shave and feel his breath on my cheek. "I'd be losing my shit if I were you, too. But, I promise we will figure it out."

My watery gaze met his confident one. "I feel safe with you, Ray," I whispered. "When I'm here or near you, I feel like that's true."

He pulled the chair closer, leaned into me so he was once again an inch from my face.

"I want you to feel safe, Andy."

I didn't know why I felt so bold but suddenly I did. Perhaps it was desperation.

"Is that all you want me to feel?"

"Oh, Andy," he said right before his lips crashed against

mine. The surge of lust was insane, and suddenly I was being hoisted up, my back pressed against the kitchen table.

"I'll make you feel so much more." His voice was gravelly and deep, and I closed my eyes when he began to suck on my neck.

I hope he didn't regret this later.

12

RAY

The entire time I walked the aisles of the grocery store I'd thought about this. The softness of Andy's lips, his slender body pressed completely to mine, and I was no longer strong enough to resist. I straightened and Andy watched me, there was insecurity in his gaze and I didn't like it. I removed his t-shirt to expose perfect, creamy skin.

Resistance wasn't an option.

I lowered my upper body until I took Andy's mouth again. As he moaned, I pushed my tongue past his parted lips, and his hands clawed at the back of my shirt. We rutted together. I stroked his skin, savored the silkiness of it and realized I could quickly become addicted to him.

When I broke the kiss, he arched his neck and I took the invitation. I bit and sucked at his throat. He whispered my name and his need was clear in the single syllable. I hooked my left hand under Andy's knee and caressed upward until I squeezed one handful of ass cheek. When I sucked roughly at one nipple, Andy's body violently arched and a chuckle worked its way up from deep in my chest.

I froze as he stiffened and lifted my head enough to take in the odd expression on his beautiful face.

I stopped everything and rested my forearms on either side of Andy's head. Stroking his soft hair as I tried to analyze what was wrong. The young man's eyes were squeezed tightly shut.

"Andy, what's wrong, come on, baby, look at me. Second thoughts?"

Andy shook his head, but still refused to look at me.

"This stops now unless you talk to me."

The threat worked and Andy's pale blue eyes met mine.

"Good boy, now, talk."

"I'm kinda skinny, men like...I'm skinny and clumsy."

"Bullshit. Wrap your legs around me."

He did as I said and I picked him up to carry him to my room. I didn't know how far Andy was ready to go, but to be on the safe side I wanted to be near supplies. I kissed him between steps and whispered words. Andy's insecurity shocked me. He was beautiful and to me just right.

When I stopped at the end of my bed, I used one hand to loosen his embrace around my neck. He tumbled to the bed with a squeak.

"What the hell was that?"

I didn't answer, just raised my arms to grab the back of my shirt and pull it off. I'd never exactly been one of those ripped guys men lusted after. I bent over to remove my boots, then stretched back to my full height.

"Now, let's clear up a few things, you're fucking perfect from your shaggy black hair to the tips of your toes. If anyone needs to worry about what someone is going to think, it's me."

Since Andy was uncomfortable, I had to change tactics. I'd love on him until he didn't remember any stupid ass insults. I slowly stripped him without breaking eye contact, and finally, he was naked and spread out across my bed.

"Scoot up the bed."

Andy moved until his head rested on my pillow. I crawled onto the bed and then sat back on my heels.

I placed my hands on his inner thighs and kneaded the tensed, slender muscles. I bent and nuzzled his balls with my nose, then dragged the tip along the slender length of Andy's hard cock. I couldn't help groaning at the scent of him. Andy's hips arched off the bed, and his fingers tangled in my hair. I sucked at the broad head, tongued the leaking slit, and then I swallowed him to the back of my throat.

Andy fit just right, the texture of his cock teased my tongue and without giving him time to adjust, I bobbed along his length. I gripped his hips until I knew I'd leave fingertip bruises. He squeezed my head with his strong thighs. Our grunts synced and I tore at my belt and the front of my jeans until my dick was free. The trimmed curls at the base of Andy's cock teased my nose as I swallowed around the tip until he was jerking.

I jacked my cock as I started the up and down movements again, the taste of his pre-come becoming stronger. I sucked on and off the head until I thought Andy would rip my hair out. I needed another taste of him and released him, slammed my mouth down on his. Resting my right hand beside his head, I took both our cocks in my left as I kissed him. The feel of his dick against mine was almost too much, but I wouldn't stop until I felt him come on my skin. Had his scent on me. We thrust in and out of my tight grip.

In this moment, the world faded away and it was just the two of us. Nothing existed but us and the pleasure I could bring Andy.

I rested my forehead on his, he barely got my name past his lips before I felt the warmth of his release on the hairy, curve of my stomach. I took his lower lip between my teeth and increased the pace of the jacking of our cocks until my body tensed and heated, I thrust harder and faster. My thigh muscles shook as I groaned Andy's name, and I came on Andy's flat stomach.

My seed covered hand went from our cocks to his side, rubbing it into the skin that covered his ribs. I kissed him gently until he relaxed and his breaths evened out. When I collapsed on him he held me tight as if I'd pull away, and I had no intention of doing that. I rolled until he was tucked against my side. I drew my fingers down the indent of his spine.

"We good or have the second thoughts creeped in?"

I was the type of person who wanted everything on the table. If this was a one-off tension release thing then I could deal with it.

"No, no second thoughts."

Andy combed his fingers through the thick hair on my chest.

"Good." I crossed my arm over my chest and placed my curled fingers under his chin. I made him look at me and brushed my mouth against his.

Andy fit just right against my side. Yes, I had those thoughts that this was in some ways due to stress or gratitude, but I tried not to let them bring down my mood. I was so much older than Andy, and no matter what Andy thought or said, he could have any man he wanted.

"Get your sexy ass up and take a shower, and I'll clean the kitchen." I gently poked his side.

"I made the mess," Andy lightly argued.

"You cooked." I gave his ass a sharp tap to get him moving.

Andy rolled over to the opposite side of the bed and got up. I couldn't take my gaze off him as he left my room. I laid there for a few minutes, for the first time in months, hell, years I didn't feel stress or dread.

I sat up and used my t-shirt to clean up enough to go take care of the mess in the kitchen. As I did up my zipper, I made my way downstairs. The sex didn't make me forget about the break-in or the phone call.

I'd waited for the killer to make a mistake and he was making plenty, but I still didn't understand how Andy was involved beside being a witness. I didn't understand the obsession and what Andy had that the killer wanted. If this was about me like Donnelly implied, then why not contact me. I was plenty easy enough to find. I was a creature of habit.

I swept up the broken plate and food, wiped up the floor, and then went about washing dishes. I heard the water running through the pipes and without meaning to my mind pictured Andy naked in my shower.

This was what I'd been afraid of, that when we took this step that he'd become a distraction. But that wasn't right, he wasn't a complication. The minute I met Andy at Rudy's, even before I knew he was there to see me my attraction was instant.

Andy would need to come to work with me in the morning so I could use my work computer to run the searches I needed, and then I had to call in a few favors. I was looking forward to seeing Andy's reaction to the people he was about to meet. I never thought I'd walk back into my old life, but for Andy, to keep him safe I would.

I placed the last dish in the drain beside the sink and dried my hands. I made sure everything was locked up and that I'd set the alarm. I padded barefoot upstairs and as I stepped onto the landing I caught sight of Andy exiting the bathroom. He smiled shyly and I closed the expanse between us until I could take his mouth again. His warm, damp skin pressed to mine, and he smelled like my body wash.

My control was tenuous at best as I gripped the perfect curves of his ass in my hands. I parted them and teased his tight hole with the tips of my index fingers.

"Get in bed, I'll be there in a minute."

"Tease."

"I'm only a tease if I don't come through one day. We've got an early day and you need to rest."

Andy nodded and I sent him to bed while I went to take a shower. I didn't linger because I had Andy in my bed, waiting for me, all the bullshit could wait for tomorrow. Right now, I just wanted to enjoy a night without our problems intruding.

13

ANDY

I woke the next morning to the sound of the shower. The pipes made the same low thumping noise mine did at my place. The clock beside Ray's bed read six, and I couldn't understand why anyone would be up at this hour. Maybe Ray had another client he needed to deal with.

The shower had just shut off when I finished getting dressed. I leaned against the wall by the bathroom door and couldn't help the laughter that bubbled out of me when Ray opened the door and practically yelped when he saw me.

"Did I scare you, detective?"

He smirked, and I took a second to appreciate him with just a towel wrapped around him. I liked that Ray wasn't all muscles and six packs. He was real and he was gorgeous. I'd seen those tattoos covering his upper arms and chest last night. In the morning light they stood out more. There was no other way to describe most of them other than to say gang tattoos. I'd seen some of the symbols before. Ray's past was forever etched into his flesh. A part of me wondered if he'd ever consider removing them, but Ray seemed like the type of guy that needed to be reminded what he left behind. I couldn't fault the man for his past. He wasn't a monster.

"Need the shower?" he asked as he pushed me fully against the wall, his damp skin pressed against me. Our roles were reversed from the night before.

"Um, just wanted to brush my teeth, pee, you know, human things. I was going to make breakfast, coffee...um."

He was making it hard to think being so close to me, his lips danced along my neck, and when he hummed, I felt it ripple through my body.

"I have to go to the office, we have a few places to go to today, but we have time for breakfast, coffee, and other human things." When his tongue joined in I was a goner.

"Shit, Ray, I can't think when you do that."

He lifted his head and his dark eyes were like molten chocolate. "Why do you need to think?" He took my hand and with his other, he tossed his towel. Sinfully slow he backed me into the bathroom, and I was about to ask what he was doing when he reached for the knobs on the shower.

"Didn't you shower already?"

He began divesting me of my clothes in the most sensual way I'd ever seen it done. "I'm feeling quite dirty, Andy."

When the water was steaming up the bathroom, he pulled me in and the next half-hour was the best shower I'd ever taken in my life.

IT TOOK US TWO HOURS TO GET OUT OF RAY'S PLACE AND NEITHER of us were sorry at all. He said he had a tech guy he knew, or sort of knew, and he wanted to see what he could do with the number that called me last night. So we bypassed going to his office first in favor of meeting him.

A lot of New West City was shady, but where Ray took us made shady look like paradise.

"Where are we? I've never been here before." The streets were filthy, every building was in shambles, and layers of neglect covered each street and alleyway.

"This is where people go to get lost, hide, or where the forgotten go to die." Ray's voice was a whisper, like he didn't want the dying dreams to hear him.

"Your tech friend lives here?"

I saw Ray shake his head in the corner of my eye. "Nah, he lives somewhere else, but because what he does isn't exactly legal, he hides here."

"How'd you come to work with him?" Ray intrigued me a lot. It was like he teetered on the line of good and bad. Good likely won out nowadays.

"You ever heard of Finn Mac?" he asked as he took a turn down a narrow alley.

"Who hasn't?" It was true. He wasn't Al Capone or anything, but the man was known as a crime boss and people knew not to cross him.

"Yeah, well, years ago cybercrimes got a call about some hacker. I had a partner back then and he and I were near where they located him. We went to pick him up and when we arrived, Finn Mac was there with the kid."

Ray stopped the car but didn't make a move to get out, and I was enthralled with the story.

"My partner wasn't exactly the clean sort, so when Finn offered us a thousand bucks to scram, he took it." He shook his head in a way that screamed disappointment. "I refused the money but saw how outnumbered we were with Finn's men and left."

"You're lucky to be alive, Ray." I heard a lot on the street about witnesses, hell, I was one and look how that was working out for me.

"Yeah, well, I leave Finn alone and he lets me be, but a week after that I saw him at Rudy's and he said he owed me one."

I felt my eyes widening. "So, you're cashing in, years later...now?"

He nodded. "I had to contact Finn before coming here. It's why I was up so early. He wakes with the sun and if I wanted to catch him, I had to call early."

Ray opened his door and I followed suit. "Who is this kid?"

He didn't answer me until we were standing in front of a rickety door.

"To the hacker world he's H@ck_th3oo_knıfe, hack the knife." He knocked.

"And to you and me?"

Ray shot me a look I couldn't decipher. "Benji Mac, Finn's son."

Any questions I had after that would have to wait because the door opened. Kid was a lose term. Benji looked to be my age, long black hair that was past his shoulders. His blue eyes stared at us under a furrowed brow. He was tall and broad and looked nothing like a hacker to me. More like a rocker who played football on Saturdays.

"Hey Benji," Ray said with his hand out.

"Ray, pops said you needed help." He laughed. "Gotta say it shocked the shit outta me. But then again, heard you took a bribe and aren't with the PD anymore."

"Don't believe everything you hear." Ray didn't elaborate, and I didn't ask what Benji meant. He gestured toward me. "This is Andy."

"Hey." Unlike Ray I just waved. The fact that this large man was Finn Mac's son was jarring. But I trusted Ray, so I followed him into the scary man's apartment, or hideout, and was shocked at how clean it was and by all the high-tech equipment.

"Aren't you afraid someone will break in here and steal all this?" I asked, and I got the answer when Benji just smirked at me. Right, his dad was a terrifying crime lord.

"So, whadda ya need, Ray?" Benji sat in a large black leather desk chair, arms behind his head and a smile plastered on his face.

"I need to see if you can track a number for me." That was my cue to hand over my phone.

"That's it?" he scoffed but took my phone. "Have a seat. There's beer and shit in the fridge."

Ray went to the kitchen while I sat on the sofa, declining the offer of a drink from him. Benji's hideout was luxurious. There was well over half-a-million dollars' worth of equipment in here and I felt a twinge of jealousy when I caught sight of the game station he had going on. I had my PS4 still at my apartment and made a mental note to see if we could maybe get it soon.

"This was made from a burner, Ray. Can't trace it but..." His cackle was almost maniacal.

"What, you got something?" I asked walking over to him just as Ray came out of the kitchen.

"The sellers of burner phones don't have a legal obligation to maintain records of who they sell them to. That's why they're called burner phones," Benji said as he scrolled over foreign data on a screen in front of him.

"So, you have nothing?" Ray asked as he sipped a beer.

"No. I have something." He clicked over the keyboard and another monitor next to him lit up. "There." He pointed to what looked like a map. "I was able to trace the call to that cell tower."

"So they were near there when they called." I moved closer to see the location. "Is it weird that that cell tower is right near where Elise lives?"

"I'd guess a sale was made at a convenience store near there. Most people buy burners, use them, and discard." Benji's fingers raced over the keyboard. Monitors were lighting up and I had no idea what I was seeing.

"I'd go talk to the person who owns that place." He pointed to the same store I bought boxers at the other day. "Someone bought six burner phones from there same day and time. No others in the area did. Your guy is getting ready for some serious communication."

"Damn, you're good," I said reverently. I was seriously impressed.

"Thanks." Benji winked and Ray cleared his throat.

"They'd remember selling that many phones to one person, and if they don't, they're lying," Ray said as he patted Benji's shoulder. "Thanks."

"We're even now, Ray."

Ray placed his empty beer bottle on the table and nodded. "We are. Come on, Andy, we have a clerk to talk to."

14

RAY

The building we entered was one of those family owned stores that survived on loyalty rather than those commercialized franchises. They were the neighborhood one-stop shop. Andy was close behind me. He'd handled meeting Benji better than I thought, but we had a few more stops today. I wondered what he'd think about the world I was more comfortable in and how he saw that meshing with me as a former cop. Benji bringing up the career ending frame-up for the bribe made me anxious, and I wondered when Andy would start to ask questions.

A tall thin guy with a comically rounded beer belly stood up from behind the counter. He was chewing on a stubby, fat cigar.

"Hey, name's Ray Clancy, I'm a private investigator. I wanted to ask you about a recent purchase. You got a minute?" I asked as I stopped, and Andy moved to my side.

"I might."

"Someone purchased several prepaid phones, I was wondering if we could look at the surveillance videos."

"It's a twenty-four-hour loop, those things overwrite themselves every day."

Shit, just what I needed. A lot of smaller shops hadn't upgraded to twenty-first century equipment, hell, I'd worked enough robberies to know some of the cameras were dummy ones with a watch battery to run the red recording light.

Another complication and I had to hope this guy had a long memory.

"Well, do you remember the person, maybe a description?" I asked.

"Do you know how many people come in here every day, man?"

"How many come in to buy several phones at once?" I was getting agitated.

"Guy came in, but in this neighborhood, you don't ask questions."

"Tall, short, my age, younger?" I asked.

I didn't know what I expected. A half-assed description would be better than nothing.

"If I remember right, wasn't a big guy. Kinda soft looking. He wasn't chatty. Paid in cash, wallet was fat."

"You see him around before?"

"No, only time. He had a baseball cap and kept his head down."

Again, not helpful, but if the guy wasn't a regular then that would mean this wasn't his home turf. I'd held out some hope that the killer lived in the area because at least that would narrow down our search.

"Any distinguishing marks, tattoos, maybe a scar?"

"None of those either. Just a guy, man, nothing special. Like about a dozen other people who come through here every day."

I thanked him, placed my hand on Andy's lower back, and led him back outside.

"That wasn't helpful."

I chuckled at Andy's frustrated tone.

"You wouldn't make a good cop. Patience is a virtue. Well, I can't fault you too much I don't have many virtues. We're going to ask about the newest vic. I know a few people in the building."

"You did this for a living?"

I couldn't hide my amusement. "Baby, not all police work is like what you see in those TV shows. It's a lot of hit and miss."

"Clancy, you back on the streets, man?" Jules Monahan, an old informant of mine, called from his spot on the steps where he smoked.

"Jules, you still on the streets?"

"My old lady told me one more stint and I could pack my shit. You know she's the only one who can put up with me. I'm straight-ish."

I nodded, "Jules, this is Andy, Andy, this is Jules."

I waited while they exchanged greetings, and I stole a glance at Andy. I could see the curiosity intensifying and knew I was going to have to answer some questions when it was just the two of us. Again, I was a good cop, never took any bribes or looked the other way unless it would benefit me later. Like I did with Finn and Benji.

"He don't look like a cop."

"No, he's a client I'm helping out with a little something."

Andy's sudden tension would've gone without notice if I hadn't paid closer attention. But to be honest, what was I supposed to say? It was one night and I didn't know what to call Andy. Whatever my personal feelings, I'd prefer if rumors didn't start circulating, especially about a relationship between me and Andy. I was well-liked but that didn't mean I didn't have enemies, and perps loved to hold grunges. I'd make it right later.

"Any newcomers to the neighborhood?" I wanted to get away from Jules' focus on who Andy was.

"Other than then the killer that murdered the guy in the

apartment above mine, not that I've noticed. Did see a guy hanging around a few times before though. About your boy's height." I rolled my eyes at Jules waggling his brows. "Softer though. Didn't look like no criminal. Jeans and t-shirt, baseball cap. Had some logo on it."

The clerk mentioned a baseball cap, but the guy hadn't mentioned a logo, so I was interested if Jules remembered anything.

"Recognize it?"

"Naw, man, some sort of generic thing."

"Remember anything else?"

"He knew where all the cameras on the street were. A few years back, you know they upgraded that shit all big brother. He kept his head down. I wouldn't have noticed at all..." Jules paused.

I made note of that and wondered if Benji would help me out with hacking into the cameras. If nothing else, I could get a general description and maybe the guy fucked up. Maybe would give us even a glimpse of his profile. You could also tell a lot about a person by how they moved—held themselves.

"What caught your attention?" I asked.

"I got a little paranoid. Between you and me, I pulled a job last month and, well, I thought he might be an undercover, but after watching him for a few days, I don't know."

"Have you seen him again?"

"Not since Chad got taken out."

"Chad, what can you tell me about him?"

"Kid should've had a revolving door on his apartment and he didn't seem too particular. Although, there was this one, damn, I woulda taken that one for a ride. Seemed to be Chad's favorite."

"What about that one?"

Jules laid out a perfect description, and I made mental notes to put in my notebook later. "Don't know, like one of those too good-looking motherfuckers. He definitely wasn't from around here. Been coming by for a few weeks maybe. He didn't give us mere mortals much attention when he came to see Chad. Although, walls and shit are thin around here, they did have an argument and the door slammed. About three hours later, that's when the cops showed."

That didn't work with the time of death and the shitty response time. Donnelly told me Chad was only dead about an hour prior to the discovery of the body.

"Did you hear anything between the door slamming and the cops coming?"

"Not really, man. Sounded like the dude might have come back for one helluva rage bang, but it wasn't unusual. Chad seemed to like it rough. My old lady complained enough about the noise from upstairs. After a while, you know you start ignoring that shit. Around here, we mind our own business."

"Anybody I should talk to?"

"Mrs. Jenkins, she lives across the hall, and you know that woman is nosy as fuck."

Mrs. Jenkins was an elderly lady who lived in the same apartment for fifty years. Every person in the neighborhood feared her and she didn't take any shit.

"Thanks, man."

"That was fucked up shit that went down when you left the force. You were hard-assed, man, but fair."

I brushed it aside as quickly as possible and made my way inside, Andy right behind me. I opened the old-fashioned lattice work metal doors of the elevator.

"That's the second time I heard about you leaving the force."

"I was framed for taking a bribe."

"They actually thought you did it?"

I didn't know what to say for a minute. Everyone instantly thought I was guilty, even my friends had looked at me with suspicion. He barely knew me and he had more faith in me than I did myself. When I opened my mouth to speak the words wouldn't come, but I cleared my throat and took a deep breath, then forced them out. "Thanks for believing me without an explanation."

"Maybe you can tell me later, when we go home?"

"Definitely."

In the privacy of the elevator, I grabbed Andy around the waist and pulled him flush to me. I gave him a quick kiss, it was supposed to be quick, but as soon as the curves of his lips gave under mine, I gave in to deepening the kiss. Memories of the night before and the shower this morning came back to me. I groaned as I forced myself to release him. Every small smile Andy gave me tempted me to taste him.

"Just a little longer and we can go back to the house. I know this isn't fun for you."

"I'm having fun and I'm not trapped in the house or apartment. Not to mention you have some interesting friends."

"I did say I wasn't always on the straight and narrow, but I'll tell you all about it later.

The conversation with Mrs. Jenkins took longer than I'd planned because she'd insisted on making us tea. She was like a lot of elderly ladies I knew from New West's rougher areas. Hard as nails, but wanted to make sure you were fed. I let her fuss over Andy and me, she pretty much repeated everything Jules had.

I thanked her, and we left; half-hour later we were pulling up to a brownstone.

"Who lives here?"

"Come on, I want to introduce you to a few people."

The door opened, and a big bruiser of a guy stepped out onto the stoop. As always, the guy had a don't fuck with me expression. I exited the car and walked around to open the door for Andy. I ascended the steps, squaring my shoulders and waiting for a fight.

"What the fuck you doing here? You ain't got no badge, so, you ain't got no business with the boss."

Richie Callaghan crossed his thick arms over his broad chest. Andy was peeking around my shoulder as I stopped in front of the bald, mean looking man.

"Do I gotta kick your ass again?" I asked.

A big fist connected with his shoulder and Richie snorted. "Man, you ain't kicked my ass since we were sixteen. Boss, didn't say you were coming around?"

"Surprise visit, I'm calling in a favor."

"You're doing that a lot lately."

I didn't like the arrogant smirk on Richie's face.

"Didn't think there was a time limit."

"Get your ass in here, boss is out back."

I grabbed Andy's hand and laced our fingers. I gave it a reassuring squeeze as we walked through the brownstone which was decorated with the richest of tastes. Shit, I hesitated walking on the area rugs or leaving a scuff on the dark hardwood floors.

Thankfully, the door for the back patio was open and I walked through it.

"Ray, what a pleasant surprise." The man I came to see stood wearing a broad friendly smile.

Even casually dressed, Theodore Bradford was an imposing man. He exuded a power that not many could come close to. While Finn was happy running downtown, Bradford aimed to control it all and did. I had a respect for the man. I worked for him in my teens and early twenties when he was just starting out. Bradford had everyone in his pocket from beat cops to the mayor.

"How you doing, Bradford?"

"Can't complain, please, come and have a seat. Can I get you and your...friend something to drink? Maybe something to eat?"

I gestured Andy into one of the patio chairs and took the seat beside him as I introduced him to Bradford. Everyone knew who he was, and Andy looked shocked. Bradford's housekeeper poured Andy and I coffee.

"So, I'm sure this isn't a friendly visit, what can I do for you?"

"You heard about the killer that's targeting young men?"

"Who hasn't? The cops are being obtuse as usual. Weren't you working on a similar case before you left the force?"

"Yeah, Andy's roommate was one of the victims, and he's being targeted for witnessing whatever. I can't keep my eyes on him all the time."

"I can take care of myself, Ray."

I caught Andy glaring at me with a stubborn tilt to his chin. Of course, I didn't mean to act as if I didn't think Andy could take care of himself, but this was what I did.

"I know, I really do, but this would make me feel better. Can you please do this for me?"

Andy nodded, but I knew that wasn't the end of the conversation. Andy was in a fucked-up situation, but he was a strong-willed man. That didn't change the fact Andy was in danger, and I couldn't leave him unprotected when I had to go places he couldn't. The phone call was enough to show me that whoever the killer was he wasn't going to stop until he found Andy.

"You know how I feel about you and the loyalty you've shown over the years. I'll send Richie to watch your young man's back, and my home is always open to you."

"I appreciate that, Bradford."

"Explain the situation to me."

And I did, I told Bradford what I knew, and he asked Andy questions, too. It was getting late and I accepted the invitation to dinner even though I just wanted to take Andy home. Bradford was doing me a solid. Even with the favor, Bradford didn't have to help me. My association with Bradford afforded me a level of protection, but that didn't seem to work with the man who targeted the young men of New West. It wouldn't stop the killings; the only thing that would end those was to find the killer however I could.

15

ANDY

The following morning while I was sitting in the kitchen nursing a cup of coffee Ray told me he was going to meet Finn Mac to see if he could talk to Benji about the street cameras.

"I just need fifteen minutes to get dressed and we can go," I said as I went to the sink to pour the rest of my coffee out.

"No." Ray's voice was sharp. Turning I saw his eyes go soft. "Sorry, I didn't mean to snap at you. Look." He stepped into my space. One hand touched my cheek, the other my shoulder. "I'm not sure bringing you all over the city while I ask hardened criminals and shystee strangers questions is exactly keeping you safe. Theodore Bradford has generously given me Richie when I'm in need of him, and I exposed you to people I probably shouldn't have yesterday."

I couldn't help the laugh that burst from my mouth. "The hulking and terrifying looking guy that practically set me on fire with his eyes? I'm supposed to feel safer with him by myself?"

"Yes." Ray spoke in a way that brokered no argument. "If you fear him others fear him, and they should. There's not a lowlife, executive, or cop who doesn't know Richie Callaghan and who he works for. Fucking with you while you're with Richie would be a grave mistake for anyone."

Part of trusting Ray was trusting who he allowed around me and where he took me. He didn't feel comfortable taking me to see Finn Mac or back to the dilapidated part of the city. That was evident in his expression.

"Okay, Ray."

"Thank you." He gave me a chaste kiss before walking out of the kitchen to finish getting ready.

Even though I wasn't joining him, I still took a shower and got ready for the day. I didn't think going out would be a great idea, and when Richie arrived, I didn't want to just be in my boxers.

I was ready to argue with Ray when we got home last night about his need to have a babysitter for me, but when he spooned behind me and thanked me for not fighting him on the protection, I melted into a pile of goo. Of course, the goo also prevented me from asking Ray more about his past.

When there was a knock on the front door, I yelped. Ray didn't laugh as I expected him to, he kissed my forehead, told me it was just Richie. I was so jumpy these days, no wonder why but sometimes my own fear of the situation got the better of me.

When Ray opened the door, I saw Richie, all eight hundred feet of him. I wondered if he had to crouch and shimmy to get through the doorway.

"Thanks for doing this, Richie." Ray patted him on his thick arm.

"I do what the boss tells me to. I'm told I gotta keep your little lamb safe. I'll do it." Richie's voice was so deep I felt the vibration through my feet.

"I shouldn't be gone long, but you never know when dealing with Finn."

I didn't miss the scowl Richie gave Ray at the mention of Finn's name. "I'm assigned to Andy until the boss says otherwise so do your thing."

My eyes followed Ray as he opened a drawer by the small table next to the couch. He pulled out one of his trusty pads and slipped it in his back pocket.

"You'll be fine, Andy, if you need me, call." He gave me a kiss and was out the door.

Richie didn't take any time at all getting comfortable. He drew all the curtains I opened, sat on the couch, and turned the television on to some sports channel. I guessed it was going to be a boring day.

WHEN NOON STRUCK MY STOMACH RUMBLED, I WENT TO THE kitchen to make lunch. I figured tomato soup and grilled cheese were good.

Richie came in just as I was placing cheese on the bread. "I was just going to order a pizza, but if you have enough I'd love some of that." He pointed to the skillet with a hopeful expression.

"I have plenty, have a seat it won't take long."

"So, you saw your friend get killed?" Richie wasn't a pillow talker, his brash question made that clear.

"Yeah. His name was Francis. Good guy." I wouldn't say it got easier talking about Francis' murder, but I was no longer fooling myself that I could hide from talking about it. I slipped two grilled cheese onto a plate and brought them over to Richie, followed by a bowl of soup.

"Ray figure anything out?" he asked as he shoved almost an entire half of sandwich in his mouth. Did he not realize it was hot?

"I think right now all we can be certain about is that it's not a woman. Everyone who saw a glimpse of him confirmed that. When I saw him, I was too terrified to take anything in except that my friend was being butchered." The hunger I felt a moment ago began to dissipate with the memories of Francis' death, talking and remembering were drastically different. I sat across from Richie, my own food now getting cold.

"It may not seem like much, but knowing that eliminates a lot of fucking people." Richie's expression was hard. Impenetrable even. I couldn't tell what he was thinking or feeling just looking at him.

"I guess." I scooped up some soup and slowly began eating.

"I'm surprised Ray didn't ask my boss to poke into the police reports or dig into the underground. If there's a killer ripping apart young men, I have no doubt my boss is looking into it. Might want to tell Ray that while I'm a good favor to ask for, there are better ones my boss can give him."

I didn't put it past Ray to have thought about that. One thing you learn living how we do is the more valuable the favor the more soul sucking the return.

"I'll tell him."

We ate the rest of our lunch in companionable silence. Only when I was loading the dishwasher did Richie leave me with a passing thought.

"And I'm not a detective or nothing, but maybe start getting curious about Ray's ex-partner?"

It seemed Richie's looks were deceiving. He looked like brainless muscle, but he was far from it. I made a mental note about talking to Ray about these things when he returned home.

Ray didn't get home until close to six in the evening. He

was disheveled, and he looked frustrated which told me he hit walls.

"I'm assuming it didn't go well?" I asked after Ray shut the door behind Richie. Both agreed he'd return in the morning.

"Finn gave me the okay to talk to Benji again, and he was able to hack into the cameras." Ray tossed his keys in the bowl and ran his fingers through his hair. "This guy, I could see him. Everything about him told me he knew what he was doing. His head was down the whole time, generic cap, he gave nothing away."

Frustration got the better of Ray and he kicked the laundry basket, spreading the clothes along the floor.

"Sorry," he said as he began picking things up.

"Don't worry about it. Richie ordered Chinese for dinner, why don't you go in the kitchen and have some. I have things to ask you."

"I ate some pizza. Just ask, Andy, just ask."

I made quick work of tossing things back into the basket while Ray took his shoes off and sat on the couch.

"Richie isn't an idiot," I started, pulling a chuckle from Ray.

"Never said he was."

I sat beside him and continued, "Why didn't you ask Theodore Bradford to help you dig into what the police know, or find out what he already might know about the killer?"

"Why would I? He's not my secretary. And he knows I'm working on it if he knew something I'm sure he'd tell me."

He had a point but... "Yeah, but men like him like to have men like you owe him."

I watched as Ray scratched his day long scruff, squinting in thought. "I can bring it up, but I won't sell my soul for it."

I nodded, accepting that. "I have one more question to ask you tonight, Ray."

"Shoot." He smiled, more relaxed as we decompressed from the day.

"Tell me what happened to your partner."

16

RAY

I appreciated Richie taking care of Andy for me. Andy also picked up on Richie as more than some hired muscle. Andy had great instincts. All day, Andy had been close to my thoughts, and I'd worried if he was okay. Andy was quickly taking up more and more of my attention, and I'd looked forward to coming home for the first time in years.

It was a fucked-up day and I still didn't feel any closer to an answer or suspect. Was it shitty of me to enjoy the act of being back on the job? I missed being a cop and helping people that needed me. Andy sat beside me on the couch, and I slipped my arm around him to hug him to my side. I'd anticipated Andy's curiosity, and I relaxed waiting for it. When Andy asked about my former partner, I wondered where it came from.

"Partner?"

"Richie said to start getting curious about your ex-partner."

"C.B. Daniels, he was my only long-term partner. No one really wanted to work with me."

"Why?"

I'd already explained some of it, but maybe Andy needed more detail.

"The old-timers on the force remembered me from when I ran the streets. Rumors were I still had friends in some pretty low places. And I did. I ain't going to lie. I don't hide my past and I'm not proud, but I ain't ashamed either. I thought I was big and bad back then, invincible."

"Were you?" Andy asked, and laughed.

"I sure as hell thought so."

"So they didn't like you for that?"

I only sensed Andy's curiosity and I liked that he wasn't judgmental.

"I was dirty by association, but I was a good cop and I worked my ass off to prove myself. When I made detective, they assigned me and Daniels as partners. Good guy, or so I thought."

"Is he the one who took the bribe from Finn?"

"Yeah, up until that point we were cool. We'd have beers after work. Hang to watch games or whatever at one of our places. Not exactly friends, but I trusted him to watch my back until I didn't anymore."

I raised my hand to comb my fingers through Andy's hair as I tried to get my thoughts together. I turned my head to kiss his forehead. I didn't understand why Richie brought up C.B., but I knew Richie wasn't a fan of the guy. Although, Richie didn't like many people I knew of, and he'd rather kill than talk to most of them.

"C.B. was one of those guys that people liked but didn't know why they liked him. I'd always found him a bit of a braggart. Always had a girl he'd been out with the night before. I don't think he was as popular as he made out."

"Is he the reason you lost your job?"

Andy rubbed my chest and I grabbed his hand to bring it to my lips. I brushed a kiss to his knuckles. I placed his hand back where it had been and stroked my fingers along his forearm as I gathered my thoughts.

"No, I was working the original case, we'd just found the third body and my Captain showed up on the scene. Told me Internal Affairs was waiting for me. I get there and they accuse me of taking a bribe. Showed me pictures of someone who was about my general age and size making a deposit into my account. It was all bullshit, but they were going to charge me with a felony. I took some deal, lost my job and ended up trailing cheating spouses."

"I'm sorry."

"No reason to be sorry. There was no way I could've won in court. At least with the deal I could keep my gun."

"Did you ever think the set-up had to do with the case?"

"I didn't think so, but I was getting insistent that we had a serial. The M.E. and I agreed. But just like the recent cases, they're covering it up. I just don't know why they're fighting this so fucking hard or why they'd want to take me out."

"Could it be a cop?"

That's a question I'd asked myself a dozen times. It would fit. Maybe it was too easy. It wasn't unheard of that cops committed some of the most brutal crimes, but a spree that went on this long, someone would've put it together.

"Before I left the force I would've said yes, but the recent murders are sloppy as fuck. A cop would know better."

"But whoever he is, he hid his face, knows how not to get caught. Why do you think he's getting sloppier?"

"I think he's getting more unhinged. The cops aren't acknowledging his work and he's getting desperate."

I was trying to keep my frustration in check. Yes, I wanted to find the killer and get him off the streets. Yet more than that, I wanted to make sure Andy was safe.

"Does desperate mean more dangerous? And what about the phone call, what if I was always the target and not Francis?"

I hated the crack in Andy's voice. I crossed my arm over my

chest, placing my fingertips on his cheek to turn his gaze to mine.

"I know, I know, there's so many what-ifs. I promise you, I'll keep you safe."

"Don't make promises, Ray." Andy's voice was soft.

With a nod, I let it go.

"I need to get my hands on the official files. My notes only give me so much and what if his M.O. has changed."

"You don't have any friends left? Someone who might let you peek at the files?"

"Donnelly lets me have a look at his reports and passes on as much information as he can. But I don't see the forensics or the crime scene photos. I'm only getting secondhand witness statements."

My phone rang where I'd dropped it on the table beside the door earlier. Andy moved away when I got up. The caller ID read unknown caller.

I connected the call and lifted it to my ear. "Clancy."

"Turn on the news."

Bradford's command came unexpectedly, so I told Andy to turn on the TV. The crowd of reporters stood outside an apartment in a richer part of New West. I watched Andy scoot to the edge of the couch, and then I brought my attention back to the chaos on the screen.

"A spokesperson for the New West Police department and mayor's office has blocked off all of Hamilton Avenue. During the impromptu press conference, they wouldn't take any questions and any inquiries were met with 'no comment.' Does this newest crime have anything to do with the string of murders of young men that have recently frightened the residents of the city? If so, the police of our city aren't talking. We will keep a close eye on this developing story."

It wasn't the reporter that held my attention. It was the blood covered man in the background who seemed inconsolable—Captain Green. This was getting more fucked up by the second, and I knew in my gut they'd gone after the one thing you don't mess with—a cop's family, or in this case, lover.

"You and your man come see me tomorrow. I did a bit of searching on my own and, well, we need to speak."

Bradford's tone to anyone else would appear an invite for a friendly visit, but I didn't miss the order. No one denied Theodore Bradford.

"I'll have someone on your house tonight, and they'll escort you here after breakfast."

"We'll see you in the morning." I disconnected the call.

"Another one," Andy asked.

"Bradford seems to think so. I think I know who the newest victim is."

"Who?"

"Green's side piece."

This was quickly going to spiral out of control. If the killer wanted to cause a scandal, than this was the way to do it. Everything was in Green's name, from rent to bills to the credit cards the kid carried around. This exposed one of the most respected members of the New West Police Department. They'd protect their own like they always had and that meant the streets weren't safe. Finding the murderer just got that much more difficult.

The rest of the night, my mind wouldn't shut down, and even as Andy curled up next to me, I still couldn't turn it off. I played every scenario out from beginning to end and none of them felt right. Why would the killer go after Green's lover? It didn't make sense. I was sure the killer chose his victims and studied them, learned their routines, so the guy had to know who he'd targeted.

This newest move would bring the whole of city law enforcement down on him. Would they continue to deny the murders were committed by the same person or warn the young men of New West to be on the lookout?

17

ANDY

Not knowing what time Bradford would be sending someone, Ray had set his alarm for five A.M. After breakfast? I always wondered why people said that. Breakfast for me is like eleven in the morning. What if he eats at seven? Ray and I joked about it and in the end, he said five was a safe bet.

We showered, ate, and watched the news where they spoke some more about the murder. His name was Gideon Meadows. I wondered if that was his real name, but Ray didn't know. From what the reporters could piece together, his murder was exactly like Francis' and the others.

At nine there was a knock on the door. Richie and two other equally large men stood there.

"We're here to make sure you don't get dead on your way to Mr. Bradford's," Richie said with a smirk, but the redness in Ray's complexion told me he would have hit him if he wasn't in a rush to hear what Bradford had to say.

The ride was quiet; I shot a text off to Elise that I was okay, and she said she was staying at her sister's until this killer was behind bars. I told her I wasn't sure when I'd get back to work, but she said Gabin and Augustine had been so wrapped up in their collapsing marriage neither had mentioned it. I suppose that was good for now.

Richie instructed us to wait to get out until the area was secure. The whole thing felt like it was out of a movie. Aside from the phone call... and yeah, the murder of my best friend, the killer hadn't contacted me. He didn't strike me as a sniper either. Likely, all this was overkill, but I let the boys have their fun.

"I don't see you for months and suddenly we see each other twice in one week," Bradford said as we entered the fancy brownstone.

"I wish it were under better terms." Ray guided me into the living room while Bradford watched us with great interest.

"I won't beat around the bush, Ray. After you left, my concern over this issue became far too great. I have a few, shall we say, dalliances. All of them are around the age and description of these men who are being slaughtered. While none of them are more than an amazing night, I am fond of them." He sat in a wing back chair across from Ray and me. His hair was pitch black and slicked back. His eyes almost shined like silver, but it was his cockiness that shockingly gave him a rather gorgeous appeal.

"And you found something out?" Ray handed me a mug of coffee Bradford's housekeeper—maid, whatever—brought in.

"I have." Bradford's eyes shifted between Ray and me. "Andy, have you ever gone to Epiphany?"

His question seemed out of the blue. "Once maybe. It wasn't... isn't really my thing. I'm not very coordinated. Walking is hard enough, dancing is out of the question." When I looked at Ray, he narrowed his eyes. I knew he hated when I said anything negative about myself, but I wasn't insulting myself. I was not a good dancer.

"Hmm..." Bradford sipped his coffee. "Gideon Meadows,

Captain Green's little whore, was a frequent flyer over there. One of my boys knew him well." He placed his coffee down and took out his phone. "I knew to contact you about the murder because it was my boy who called me when he saw reporters begin to descend on Gideon's place."

"Your boy, who clearly is nameless, how'd he know they were going to his place? It was an apartment building," I said earning a glare from Bradford. I knew I was being snippy, but it was all cloak and dagger stuff with these guys.

"My boy, who does have a name but it's none of your business, lives in the same building. He saw the cops, the news, everything. He called me. Happy, Andy?" His tone wasn't so much sarcastic as it was annoyed. Ray's smile wiped away the nerves that I'd just upset Bradford.

"Go on." Ray pointed to Bradford's phone. "What did your concubine say?"

"Don't you start." Bradford's tone was light. "I spoke with him for a while and asked if he saw Gideon leave with anyone last night. He said he did. A gentleman who wore a fedora, a long leather coat, and he had some facial hair. He told me he'd seen him in Epiphany before." Bradford put his phone down and looked at us with slight concern.

"What is it, Bradford?"

"The man doesn't match the description of the man who was in the store or in the other apartment that killed Chad. Nor does he sound like the man who killed Andy's roommate."

There was a simple explanation to that. "So, maybe this guy isn't the killer. Maybe he was just interested in Gideon."

Bradford nodded. "I thought that as well. Then my boy explained he'd seen him before. A couple times actually. And all the men he left Epiphany with were all victims of this killer."

It felt like someone slowly poured ice water down my back. It was shocking and numbing.

"So what you're saying..." I began to say, but Ray cut me off.

"We're not dealing with one killer, we're dealing with two."

"Seems so," Bradford said. "I've told my boys to steer clear of Epiphany. It's clearly the hunting ground, but you knew that already. I can tell you something else, Ray, something you'll be glad I told you now so you will have some time to let it toss around in your brain."

"What's that?"

"With the death of Gideon, Captain Green has become fierce with his department. He has brought close to everyone in on this case. I heard through the grapevine he's actually requesting you be brought back in."

"Me, why?" Ray was surprised, but he was an idiot. Of course, they wanted Ray back. He was brilliant and he knew this case better than any of them.

"My guess is you'll find out why soon. But everything this killer, or killers, have done has one thing in common."

What's that?" I asked.

"Ray." Bradford's smile was sympathetic. "Something tells me Green knows that, and you're being brought to be what they need to make this end."

Ray didn't talk all the way back to his apartment. Richie and another man came back with us and neither of us argued, they'd be around watching out for us whenever they could, but Bradford also had to keep eyes on his lovers, too. It was dangerous out there, and if Bradford was right, Ray was important to these killers.

We'd just entered the apartment when the phone rang. Ray answered it while I put our coats away.

"Good afternoon, Green." It was all Ray had to say; Bradford was right and Ray was being thrown into the trenches.

18

RAY

The call with Green was brief, just an order issued and a time for me to be there. If I wasn't so interested in the case, I would've told him to kiss my ass. Andy held my hand tighter as we were escorted to the squad room. I'd tried to get him to stay with Richie or Bradford while I had this meeting, but Andy's tone when he said no warned me I wouldn't get my way without a fight.

I shook my head as I entered the room and saw the boards set up with each victim, even the previous ones from before I was fired. So, they weren't as sure as they played it to the press that a serial wasn't terrorizing New West, or suddenly they got their shit together. I was leaning toward the latter.

"The Captain is waiting for you in his office." The clipped tone of the young uniformed officer made me roll my eyes. His gaze was taking in my and Andy's laced fingers. I dismissed him without a glance and made my way to Green's office. The amount of ass kissing Green did to get this job disgusted me. It wasn't a job I'd wanted, but there were more qualified people that should've gotten the promotion.

Green's hair was stuck up in every direction as the man ran

his fingers through it repeatedly. To me it looked like he'd aged a decade overnight and I wasn't sympathetic. He'd brought this shit on himself.

"Clancy."

"Green."

The man snarled as he motioned toward Andy and I sensed whatever was about to come out of his mouth was going to piss me off.

"I didn't think I asked you to bring your toy with you. A little young for you, isn't he?"

"How's Gideon?" I asked.

Green's face turned, well, green, and I didn't care. The bastard had made ten years of my life hell.

Andy pinched my side and I turned my head. He had that cute expression on his face he got every time I did something annoying.

"Ray, be nice."

I knew he wasn't any fonder of Green than I was, but he knew this was my one shot at getting my hands on the evidence.

"No need for me to be nice. If Green's balls weren't in a vice at this very moment, then I wouldn't even be here. He needs me a helluva lot more than I need him."

Andy nudged my ribs with his elbow, and he took a seat without waiting for an invite. I stayed standing.

"Close the door, Clancy."

I did as Green asked and crossed my arms over my chest as I waited for him to start talking. Every minute that went by was a waste of precious time. How close were they to finding the next victim?

"I know I'm an asshole and you don't like me, but we're getting nowhere on this fucking case. You got contacts we'll never have and, as much as it pains me to ask, I need you to come back." Green's shoulder slumped and all the fight left the man.

I had a moment of pity. Maybe Green's feelings went beyond Gideon being the man's toy. I'd met plenty of closeted cops in my years, and Green genuinely seemed devastated by Gideon's murder.

"I don't have a badge anymore."

"I cleared it with the bosses, you're back on a consulting basis only."

A part of me was happy just to be back, and the other more dominant part was disappointed. I'd given my life to the force and they'd discarded me so easily. I studied Andy as he watched Green and he emanated empathy. I forced the last six months of bitterness and anger away and decided to be the bigger man.

"What do you have?"

"Nothing, no forensics that match anyone in the system. No usable prints. Either this bastard is careful to wear gloves, or he wipes everything down before he leaves. For all the brutality of the scenes, he leaves nothing. No one is talking. We've hit just about every confidential informant that we have. Either they don't know anything, or they're scared."

"I have a theory."

It was by unspoken agreement that Bradford or Mac would never make it into any report—officially or unofficially. Some would think my loyalties were skewed, but Bradford had saved my ass plenty.

"We've run out of theories, proceed."

"As you know, if you've asked around, all our victims were regulars at Epiphany. I've had an anonymous tip that all of them were seen leaving the club with an unnamed suspect. But Andy received a threatening phone call. We traced the call to a store near the fifth victim's residence."

I took the seat beside Andy's and leaned forward to rest my

forearms on my knees. I paused my train of thought to check Green's receptiveness to the theory. The man seemed interested.

"When descriptions were compared, they're two separate men. I believe that the actual killer has someone who lures the victims from the club for whatever reason, with sex or drugs. Someone who fits in, who's younger or more charming. Later, after the deed is done, our killer enters the apartment through a door his accomplice has left unlocked."

I'd done a lot of thinking after speaking with Bradford that morning, and all the pieces fell into place with the news of the second perp. The way the killer entered the apartments without force. How he took the victims by surprise. I was a bit pissed with myself for not thinking of it sooner.

"You're not going to give me your sources, are you?"

"They spoke with me under the promise that I would keep them out of it. And I don't plan on breaking that promise."

"Continue."

I straightened and relaxed in the chair, without thinking about it, I laid my right hand on Andy's leg. Touching Andy seemed so natural. The only reason I noticed was Green clearing his throat. The way Green looked away like he hadn't fucked who knows how many men over the years, like he was uncomfortable with open displays of affection. Fuck him, I didn't care. I'd sensed Andy's unease the more I spoke, and I wanted to calm him—put him at ease as much as I could.

"According to the reports from the first three murders, there was evidence of consensual sex, but on examination of evidence, no used condoms were found at the scenes. We thought the killer removed the evidence as he wiped down the surfaces. He was careful, but now I believe that the partner covered his own tracks before leaving."

"What would the partner get from this?"

"Thrill. Sex. There's been partnerships like this before. One person acts as the bait and one perpetrates the crime. Some people get off on killing. Has the shrink come on to work up a profile?"

"Generic as fuck, white male, thirty to forty-five, someone who doesn't draw a lot of attention. You know, doesn't give off the psycho vibe."

"Partner is under thirty, white male. Killer fits more with the profile. An informant said the killer was careful."

"What about the cop angle?" Andy asked.

Green's face was mottled red with anger. No one wanted to think a cop was involved, and I was keeping that information to myself until I got a look at the books and the evidence. My next stop was a visit with Donnelly.

"It can't be a cop," Green vehemently protested.

"Why not? He'd know our procedures. What forensics to destroy so as not to implicate himself. If not a cop, maybe a former one."

"The profile fits you, Clancy. You're an ex-cop. You worked the first three killings."

I couldn't resist laughing and shook my head.

"Ray's been with me the last two killings." Andy's indignation in my defense made me smile.

"Clancy did say there was a partner, do I need to ask about your whereabouts?"

The threat was there in every word and no matter how ludicrous the idea, it was too close to a possibility. We didn't fit the physical descriptions, but eye witness statements were notoriously flawed. It was common knowledge that everyone perceived someone based on bias. You could ask one person what happened, and they'd give one statement while the person beside them would have a completely different one.

"I'll let that pass. Andy's life has been fucked up by this so keep your bullshit to yourself. You might not like me and you probably think I took that bribe y'all charged me with, but you know I was a good cop, whether you want to admit it or not."

"A good cop who's friends with mobsters and lowlifes. Your jacket before your eighteenth birthday was setting you up for a life of crime."

I'd never lied about my life before, and I wouldn't start now. I'm not ashamed of what I'd done, yeah, I knew it didn't fit the profile. I was raised in a loving home. Both my parents were around until my dad's death, but that didn't mean I hadn't loved the excitement of the criminal element. The adrenaline rush I'd received. I did what I did, but I'd been clean for decades.

"You want to find your boyfriend's killer, Green, then you're going to have to trust me."

"Can I ask Mr. Shay some questions?"

"You need to ask him that."

"Mr. Shay, take me through the night you came home again."

I sat there and listened, I was as enraged hearing it repeated as I was the first time Andy told me. He had come so close to becoming a number on a file and a picture on a board.

The questions were standard eyewitness inquiries. Andy didn't provide anything new, but I'd thank him later for leaving out names when Green tried to trick Andy into giving up my sources.

"How did you come to be in the care of Mr. Clancy?"

Andy glanced at me and smiled, I gave his knee a squeeze.

"When I wasn't getting help and no one was interested in finding Francis' killer, I watched the news and there was mention of the previous murders. With some research I found Ray's name. I called him, hoping he could help me—keep me safe."

"Is that what you're doing...keeping him safe?" Green aimed the pointed question at me.

The bastard didn't faze me. I could knock out his teeth

without a second of regret, so I didn't care what he thought about Andy and me. We hadn't exactly had the conversation about what was between us, and I tried not to hope for too much.

"The half-assed protection detail fell down on their fucking job. Someone broke in the apartment and left threats. What are your theories on the new messages? 'Come back to me.' And Andy received a phone call where the presumed killer said that someone was his."

Green's face went ashen and he suddenly looked way too nervous.

"What's going on?" Andy asked.

"The last three crime scenes. We suppressed evidence."

"What evidence?" I demanded.

Green produced plastic bags with red evidence seals. The writing was block style and wouldn't work for a handwriting analysis, but I read each word. My confusion grew message after message. The killer was asking for me just as Bradford had alluded. I was supposed to come back to him and a sickness built in my stomach. I'd assumed in some way the killer knew me and that he wanted to play a cat and mouse game, but the last three killings were to bring me back. There was even an image I remembered quite clearly with the date permanently etched into my mind. The one that lost me my job, but this one was from a different angle. Although, the stranger was built like me, it clearly showed that I wasn't the one making the deposit.

"What the fuck is this, Green?"

My hands shook, and Andy saved the photos and letters from being crushed in my rage.

"The photo was left at the crime scene of Mr. Shay's roommate's murder."

"You knew this and you could've brought me back."

I surged to my feet and turned away from Green. Popping

him one wouldn't accomplish anything but making me feel better. It wouldn't get me back on the case.

"It could have easily been you committing the murder to con your way back onto the force. You worked the cases. You knew the details."

"You know that's bullshit, Green. You know how many people would kill to drop my name on a murder. They would've done it in a heartbeat."

I stared out through the opened blinds. I tried to bring my anger under control, but it seethed and bubbled up from the pit of my gut. I'd paid for something I hadn't done, and they'd had the evidence to prove it.

"I'll make you a deal, Clancy, you help us find our murderer and his partner, then I'll go to the higher ups to get you reinstated and your record expunged."

It was blackmail. It was also a low blow. This past six months I'd wanted nothing more than to have this chance to get my job back, but the department was so broken did I even want to be a part of it anymore?

"I'll need access to everything." My voice sounded terrifying even to me. It was a level of anger I'd thought I'd left behind in my youth. I wanted to hurt someone—break something. I turned slowly back to Green to find Andy watching me. Andy's expression was one I hadn't seen before, and I couldn't quite interpret it.

Green pointed to the corner and I glanced in the direction to find two file boxes.

"That was made up with everything we have, including your files from the first murders. Donnelly has been instructed to give you whatever information you need, but I'm sure he would've done it without permission."

The rest of the conversation was stiff, and I clenched my jaw so much it was sore. I grabbed the two boxes and Andy preceded me out of Green's office. When we made it to my car I stowed the files in the trunk, instead of going home to dive into the cases, I led Andy across the street to the coroner's office.

"Ray," Andy's voice was quiet and tense, and the unspoken question in it was clear.

"I'll be fine. They knew I didn't take that fucking bribe and they just let it go."

Andy grabbed my arm and pulled me to a stop, tugging me into a side hallway. The dim corridor afforded us some privacy. His slender arms raised and his hands cupped my cheeks.

"But it's out there now. You can have your job back. Isn't that what you wanted?"

"I thought so..."

"What is it?"

I lowered my forehead to rest on his as I tried to calm my breathing. Andy didn't deserve my temper, and as long as it was in my power, I'd never hurt him.

"If these are the people I worked with and they could sell me out like that, can I trust them to watch my back?"

"I guess that's something you'll have to decide, but until then, they gave you the files you wanted. That has to mean something."

I nodded as I used my curled fingers to nudge his chin until he tilted his head back. This wasn't the place, but I needed this one thing. I heard his breaths quicken and I watched his gaze flit from mine to my mouth. His lips trembled and I quickly sunk the fingers of my left hand into his hair. I slammed my mouth onto his and didn't give a fuck we were a few doors down from the morgue or that anyone could see. This kiss, this brief moment, was what I required to center myself.

A clearing throat and then a chuckle broke us apart, and I turned my head to find Donnelly grinning.

"Hello, Ray. You know, the morgue really isn't the place to spice up the sex life."

"Shut up, Donnelly."

"Do I get introduced?"

"Andy, meet Donnelly, Donnelly, meet Andy."

I put distance between Andy and myself as they exchanged greetings with a brief handshake.

"You do know, I'm a helluva lot more handsome and financially secure than Ray, right?"

I grunted as Andy laughed, and I didn't like the batting lashes Andy gave Donnelly. Donnelly might look like the absent-minded professor type with his wrinkled scrubs and doctor's jacket, but he had that too handsome thing going for him. He wasn't much older than me and his wrinkles were the attractive sort, not the ones that looked like you hadn't slept in a decade.

"I think I prefer Ray, but I'll keep that in mind."

"Might be a keeper, Ray. Green called."

"Yeah, got time for some questions?"

"For you always, did you want a look at the newest body?"

I didn't miss the sick look that came over Andy's beautiful face, and I almost refused until Andy spoke up.

"Do you have an office I can wait in?"

Donnelly led us to his office and set up Andy with a mug of coffee. I dropped a quick kiss to Andy's upturned lips before we left. I spent the next hour checking out Gideon's body after we went through Donnelly's reports. The damage was so much more brutal than normal. Yes, the bodies and scenes were bloody, but every injury was normally precise and made in an almost ritualistic way. But Gideon, he suffered a lot more damage. This spoke of an anger far removed from the calculated killer I had observed from the cases I'd worked.

I'd seen him a couple of times over the last few years and the beautiful and elegant features were pulverized. Bones broken so badly that his body was misshapen.

"What the hell happened?"

"Seems our killer took out a lot of rage on this young man here. The beating was pre-mortem." As Donnelly spoke he pointed out and recounted injuries. "Every bone in his face was crushed. His ribs were broken and one had punctured his lung, and according to my findings, the genital mutilation was done while he was still alive. If the fucker hadn't finished him off, my opinion is the young man here would've died within an hour of his injuries."

"What the fuck is going on, Donnelly?"

"Ray, if this guy isn't stopped, I'm going to have a lot more occupied drawers."

I nodded as Donnelly pulled the sheet back over Gideon and slid the slab back into the wall and closed the door. I hated what this meant, our killer was losing control and when that happened, patterns changed. Before this I was sure Andy was in danger, but now that I was in the loop, I was even more determined to protect Andy. The killer was out of control and the scariest part was, he had help to feed his madness.

19

ANDY

There was no way I was going into that morgue to look at Gideon's body, and I was glad when nobody protested me staying behind. Just seeing Francis' was enough for me. In Donnelly's office I was able to see the papers Ray had been reading, and the notes the killer left on the flesh of its victims. *Where's my Ray of sunshine. Bring him back to me.* Couple those with what the killer said to me and the other notes, and it made sense.

It wasn't me the killers wanted, it was Ray, and I was an obstacle for them. That thought had me shivering so violently I almost spilled the coffee Donnelly gave me.

Ray wasn't gone very long and when he came back to the office with Donnelly, I could tell by his face he was just as shaken over all this as I was.

In the car Ray said he was going to pick up dinner and then go over the files. While I knew that time wasn't on our side, I also knew if we, namely Ray, burned out before the killer or killers were brought down nobody won.

"Can we stop one more place before we go back to yours?"

Ray gave me a side glance, shrugged and agreed. “Where did you want to go?”

“I’ll give directions. All you have to do is trust me.”

He smiled and I wanted to slide into his lap and lick his grin so badly. But he was driving and I valued my life.

Twenty minutes later I had Ray pull into the parking lot of an abandoned building.

“Andy, why are we here?” He came to a stop at the front and turned to me.

“You have to trust me, remember?” I got out and waited for Ray to follow me.

I wasn’t going through the front door because those had long ago been sealed up. I walked around back where a faded red door was. Years ago it was an employee entrance, now it was where only I went through.

“Life is stressful, Ray. Francis and I were always scraping by. We worked hard and while he was able to blow off steam by going to clubs or playing video games with me, we both often wanted to get away.” The door stuck for a second as I opened it but one more pull and it gave way.

“We didn’t have the money to take grand vacations or even rent a car to drive anywhere, so one day he and I decided to walk. We pretended we were explorers.” I shrugged and could feel my cheeks burn. “We were dorks, but it was fun. One day we were passing here and there was this girl, about nineteen, and we saw her come in here.”

I took Ray’s hand as we walked through a back room toward a set of decrepit doors.

“We scared her when we came in, and by the looks of her she was homeless. But Francis and I told her we didn’t want to hurt her. We gave her twenty bucks and told her what we were doing. She thought we were funny and the three of us became friends.”

"What happened to her?" Ray asked as we pushed through the doors to a large opening.

"She died. She left us a note one day saying while being in the oasis gave her happy moments, the pain was too much. She killed herself in front of a hospital with my number in her pocket . They called me, but I was ready for it." My heart hurt thinking of Lily. I'd lost so many people in my life, why?

"I'm sorry."

This wasn't about grieving, it was about an escape so I shrugged it off. "Come on."

I pulled Ray's hand eagerly as we entered a sectioned off area of the building. The three of us were the only ones who ever came here, so it was frozen in time from the last time we were here.

"Welcome to the Lily Pad Oasis, Ray. Where the world goes away and your imagination is your vacation," I said with flourish.

Ray pushed back the large blue tarp. I followed him in, knowing the batteries for the lighting and sound were likely still good I clicked the switch. White fairy lights surrounded the top and by the gasp Ray let out, he was amazed at what he saw.

Lily, Francis, and I spent a long time making it the perfect escape. We scavenged things, and Francis and I ended up spending some money on the place. It looked like a mini rain forest. The switch that lit the lights turned on a small water fall and a radio that played Caribbean music.

Whenever we'd came we brought food, but I wasn't expecting this so I wasn't prepared. In the center of the oasis was a huge blow up mattress. The blankets could probably stand a washing, but we were clothed so I pushed Ray onto it.

"I come here to get away, Ray. No one knows about this place. Without Lily it was hard to come here with Francis. But we had each other to remember all the good times. Now with Francis gone, the ache would've been unbearable to come back here. But you, Ray. I got this feeling it wouldn't hurt as bad with you. Together we can make it what Lily always wanted it to be. It can be our place, Ray. Our escape, our oasis."

"Wow, Andy, this place is amazing." He looked around in wonderment, all stress washed away. Exactly what I had hoped for.

"Francis and I always said that if we couldn't find each other anywhere then we didn't look here." Ray's smiled mirrored mine.

"So you're saying if I can't find you anywhere, look here?" Ray cupped my cheek, I hovered over him as he laid on the mattress.

"I think you'd find me anywhere, Ray. But yeah. I'd be here."

The sound of the water and light music echoed through the oasis in the abandoned building as Ray pulled my lips to his. He kissed me like he was owning me, and I wanted to be owned by him.

His hands caressed down my neck, over my shoulders, and I shivered as they came to rest on my jean covered ass.

"Ray," I moaned as he nipped my chin.

"I don't have any condoms or lube, Andy. I didn't know we'd be here."

"Me either."

I didn't want to ruin the moment by telling Ray I wouldn't get naked on these blankets anyway. So I pressed him to the mattress and as smooth as possible, I shimmied down his body until my face was even with the obvious bulge in his pants.

"I want you to relax, Ray, let me help you."

He ran his fingers through my hair, and the subtle nod was all I needed.

I unzipped his pants, making sure as I slipped them down I didn't expose his butt to the sheets. I just wanted his dick, and when I pulled the briefs under his nuts it was like dessert at the oasis.

I wanted it to last for him. Slowly, I licked him from bottom to top, gently sucking the head, relishing on the burst of precome that burst over my tongue.

"Jesus, Andy," Ray mumbled as his head fell back and his arms spread in sweet surrender.

I licked, sucked, and took Ray down as far as I could over and over again until his legs shook and he fisted the blankets.

"Andy," he shouted at the same time he exploded in my mouth. I devoured every drop, almost grateful for it. I knew I was falling for Ray and giving this to him was more than my body could handle, so a second later I was coming in my pants.

I don't know how long Ray and I ended up lying there on the dirty blankets staring up at the twinkle lights and relaxing to the majestic sounds. But the sun had set, and right before my lids dropped I heard Ray say thank you.

20

RAY

When the real world lured us from the little oasis Andy had shown me, the regret was overwhelming. I wanted to stay curled up there with Andy and pretend as if we weren't being stalked by killers or our lives weren't in the bastards' hands. When we made it home I unpacked the boxes and went through each file, tacking them to the boards I'd carried up from the basement. The photos were a macabre play, tacked in order, and they were all too familiar. I'd lived with these pictures for months before I'd left the force.

Rage overtook me knowing Green and others knew I was innocent for days. I didn't have time to deal with that now. What was more important was finding the killer and his partner, making sure Andy was safe.

"Shit."

I jerked my gaze to Andy, seeing the paleness of his face and the way his hands shook around the two beers he was holding.

"Sorry, I can move this to my office, but it's a bit cramped."

"It's fine. How can you look at those?"

I brought my attention back to them, took in the faces of each victim and tried to imagine what their last moments were like before their lives were violently snuffed out. The killer probably had no qualms about what he did. Maybe the guy was even proud of his work like someone who excelled at their job. I didn't know how to answer Andy without it seeming cold, but I learned the art of being detached. Until these murders, never once was I emotionally attached or invested in a case.

Yes, I felt pity and sadness for someone losing their life, especially in violence, but this was so much more than that.

I took the beer Andy handed me. "Homicide wasn't where I'd thought I'd end up. I worked Vice and Sex Crimes for nearly a decade. I find it easier to work with the dead. The rape victims, no matter what assurances I made that everything would be okay I knew it was an empty promise."

I lifted the bottle to my mouth and took a long draw. "We were taught not to make promises. That it only gave the survivors false hope." I let out a deep sigh. "Cops sit there with these people at the worst moments of their lives and we have to instill confidence that we'll find whoever hurt them or their loved ones. After a while something deadens inside us. We've seen too much or... see the devastation on their faces when the perps are found not guilty. I became...lost and hardened."

"Why did you become a cop?" Andy asked.

He moved toward the couch and sat down, curling up on one end. I followed to perch on the arm and pulled him close. His cheek rested against my ribs and I soothingly combed my fingers through his soft hair.

"Sometimes I wonder why." I took another swallow of my beer while I tried to get my thoughts in order. "Back in the day, there was this cop, his usual beat was my neighborhood. He was quick to call me over and have a talk about what I was doing. One night, I was running an errand and it was his night to patrol. I didn't know what was in the package and I didn't ask. When I was searched, I was in possession of a distributable amount of narcotics. Let's just say I wasn't underage anymore, and I was looking at ten years in prison."

"What happened?" he asked as he stared up at me.

I lowered my head to brush a kiss to his forehead.

"He made me a deal, police academy or a cell. I didn't see much choice. He confiscated what I was holding and told me to get lost. With my history, I barely got in. Today it would've been a no go. All the younger cops are coming in with college degrees and dreams of grandeur. I worked hard to prove myself, I should've taken the Sergeant's exam years ago, but I made Detective and that was fine with me."

"Do you want to go back? You probably have that option now."

"I don't know, baby, after thinking about it. Do I really want to put my life into the hands of people who I can't trust? Really, if they didn't need me, how long would they have known I was clean and just kept going on like I was guilty? I wouldn't mind staying a P.I. with some more funding, maybe start a security type company. Who knows, right now." I leaned forward to set my bottle on the coffee table, then pinched Andy's chin between my fingers and tipped his head back. "I just want to make sure you're safe."

I quickly kissed him and stroked my curled fingers down the slight stubble on his cheek. When Andy called me for help, getting involved with him hadn't ever crossed my mind, but I didn't care. I was drawn to him and it was stronger than any other man I'd met. My need had nothing to do with the case. Yes, the job had brought us together, but it wasn't why I couldn't resist him.

He wanted to say something, I could see it in his expressive eyes, but the knock on the door caused both of us to jump. I moved quickly across the room and removed my weapon from the holster hanging on the coat hooks beside the door. I motioned for Andy to go upstairs.

"Ray, really, must I stand outside in this awful neighborhood while you figure out how to shoot me?"

I rolled my eyes as Andy snorted, I opened the door to find Bradford and Richie on the porch. Bradford looked ready to go to a five-star restaurant in his ridiculously priced suit. While Richie was in his usual jeans and t-shirt, wearing a leather jacket to conceal his .45.

"What the hell are y'all doing here?"

"We were informed that you had a most interesting day at your former precinct."

Bradford didn't fool me. I'd learned to read the man years ago when he'd taken over the operation from his old man. Bradford was only a few years older than me, but we'd grown up together.

"You just want to be nosy and get details, and also look over case files like the old days."

I motioned them both inside and closed the door. Richie took off his jacket and headed for the kitchen, making himself at home when he came back with a beer. Gruff or not, he came back with bottles for us all. He took a seat in my recliner and kicked up the foot rest. He had watched Bradford's back for so many years he knew they weren't going anywhere soon.

"Andy, how are you this evening?" Bradford poured on the charm and even kissed Andy's hand.

I almost laughed at the look of near horror on Andy's face as he backed up as if Bradford was about to have a meltdown.

"Hands off, Bradford."

"So possessive, didn't take you for the permanence type. But if anyone would instill that level of alpha posturing, your young man would definitely do it."

"Are you trying to piss me off?"

Bradford removed his even more expensive cashmere trench coat and hung it up as I put my weapon away. The man was practically bouncing with the excitement of looking through case files. I thought my friend and former boss would've made a good detective. He had an eye for detail.

"Go on."

Bradford didn't wait any longer and was shifting the files and finding the earliest murder.

Andy stepped up to my side and whispered, "What is going on?"

"Bradford wanted to be a cop, but his old man thought it was below him."

"So, he's a criminal with badge envy."

Bradford scoffed, "I'm a businessman, Andy. As with any business sometimes my dealings aren't always, shall we say, legal."

Bradford didn't look up from the file as he thumbed through the pages. My friend had an acumen for puzzles. Bradford had even helped on a few cases putting clues together. The higher ups would've lost their mind if they knew one of my best assets was one of the most respected, yet, wanted men in New West.

"Come on, Andy, let's get to work."

I took Andy's hand and we took the couch while Bradford removed his jacket and tie to sit cross legged on the floor. Hours passed, and the two huge boards were quickly filling with details. The scrawls on the whiteboard a mix of my, Andy, and Bradford's handwriting.

"I'm sure you went over your enemies, but what about your admirers, Ray?"

"Admirers?" I asked Bradford.

The thought that I had admirers was a surprise to me.

"Yes, someone who showed you more attention than others.

An individual who possibly vied for your affections," Bradford explained.

I couldn't help laughing. I mean I wasn't an ogre, but I sure as hell wasn't a catch either, before or after my life as a cop. Wealth and looks weren't exactly bestowed upon me as a gift from birth. I was rough and my manner abrasive.

"I haven't exactly gone without..."

Andy huffed beside me and I patted his knee.

"But I don't remember anyone who particularly went out of their way to get me in bed."

"What about Daniels?" Richie asked.

I'd almost forgotten the man was there until he spoke.

"Daniels was an egocentric ass, but he definitely didn't give off the lusting after me vibe. If anything, he played up his skirt chasing at every opportunity. I lost track of the number of blowjobs he got while on the clock."

I didn't know what Richie's hard on for my former partner was, but I clearly remembered he hated the man on the spot. As much as I thought about it, I couldn't see Daniels as a killer. Yeah, he was hotheaded and quick to excessive force, he wasn't allergic to pocketing a bribe, but murder I couldn't wrap my head around.

Bradford spoke without looking up from the file. "Some men find that their carnal needs for the same sex an emasculating feature and macho bullshit makes them less of a target."

"Can you talk like a normal person?" Andy's question earned him laughter from me and Richie.

"Now, you're going to hurt my feelings, Andy."

Andy snorted and went right back to reading through the case file. I'd kept Francis' case away from him. It was one thing to look at one for someone he didn't know, another to see the aftermath of what happened to his friend and roommate.

"Well, you have two men working as partners. One who is

obviously skilled enough to blend into the hunting ground of a place like Epiphany and unassuming enough to lure obviously street-smart men from the club. The files show that there was evidence of consensual sex, so I'm assuming the killer didn't—"

Andy cut off Bradford with a raised hand. "What if the partner, the younger guy, talked to these men and said he had a partner, an older boyfriend or husband. They liked to have threesomes. Francis was known to have the occasional hookup with couples. Could the partner be waiting outside in a car, partner brings the victim outside and they leave together. Sex happens between the three and when all is said and done, they kill together."

I thought about it for a minute. "Plausible theory, two people cleaning up would minimize the time it took to remove evidence, but you only saw the one killer."

"Ray, Andy might have a point about something. The last three killings were more frenzied than the first three, maybe the partner is a new addition. Partner is taking advantage and getting a few perks for his part, and jealousy is getting the better of the killer." Richie kicked the footrest of the chair down. Richie stood and walked around the boards. He tapped the first three pictures.

"See, what people fuck up with the perfect crime is they add people to the mix. Either they start sending those attention seeking notes, or they slip up by keeping a trophy. Our guy successfully pulled off three murders. No evidence or witnesses." He moved to the second board. "These three were fuck-ups all over the place. Andy as a witness. Threatening calls to Andy. Images of him from the CCTV cameras, pretty useless, but they showed a general description. And we have a second witness in Jules."

"What are you getting at, man?" I asked.

"These first three murders, I don't believe they had anything to do with you. These final three were a calling out. A declaration of war. Yes, they are the same type, slim, attractive, some might even say pretty, but who do these men remind you of, Ray? It's been staring us in the face for hours."

I scanned each one slowly and tried to see where he was going with his theory. "Hold up." I was off the couch with Andy calling my name. I jogged down into the basement and searched for the case file. It was from my Sex Crime days and I opened it as soon as I found it. The face staring back at me almost took my knees out. I ran upstairs.

"Mikey Carter, twenty-three-year-old escort. Worked for one of Finn's guys. Bradford, what's was his name?"

"Gino something, he disappeared about twelve years ago. Finn found out Gino was running a prostitution operation under the guise of an escort service. You know Finn doesn't run a stable. His older sister died when her pimp let a client beat the fuck out of her for an extra hundred. Gino kept feeding Finn a line of bullshit that it was all legit."

"Mikey worked for Gino, but I let Mikey go a few times with a couple hundred. Told him to get off the streets. Sweet kid, he just didn't have many options." I removed the photo and used a pin to place it next to the others. "I got a call, I was just signing off duty. It was Mikey. I met him. That kid was fucked up, but nothing I did would get him to name names. After he stayed in the hospital a few days, I drove him to the bus station and never saw him again."

"Whatever this is, Ray, this has been going on a lot longer than six crimes."

My stomach clenched. If this was true, we had a lot more than six victims, and if this went as far back as Mikey's case, then Finn was implicated. I wasn't ready for that complication or how many more bodies were out there. Cops didn't give a fuck about a kid working a corner. How many fucking victims were sitting in cold case files?

"I need to make a phone call." I hoped Green had opened his fucking mouth and spread the news I was back. If not, I knew the guy in charge of the Cold Case Squad.

21

ANDY

Everything felt like a tornado. You knew what it was, but had no idea the destruction it would leave behind. I knew this case was eating at Ray. I knew he was beyond worried about me and what my being a witness would mean for me. But in all we'd been through dealing with these psychos, I never saw that look of utter devastation on Ray's face until he realized all these victims looked like this guy Mikey Carter.

All I knew at this point was he was an escort and he disappeared. My mind was reeling. Was he still alive? Could they find him? Would Mikey know anything? It was like hope was battling with reality, and I didn't know which was going to win.

Ray explained he had an important call to make. Worry creased his face and a glint of fear turned his soft eyes hard. Bradford said he was going home for the evening, but he would leave a man here to watch the outside and would speak with us in the morning.

As I sat on the couch, the silence was doing nothing good for my imagination, so I decided to call Elise, see how she was doing.

"Hey, Andy. So great hearing from you. How you holding up?" She sounded truly relived, and as sorry I was for getting her wrapped up in all this, I was grateful to have become closer to her.

"I dunno. It's still dangerous, but I think they may have some solid leads."

"Good. You must be going crazy not working or anything. Any idea when you'll be back?" I was already past my week off and pushing into the two-week territory. I was sure Augustine hadn't hired anyone else, Elise would have mentioned it, but I did know how tired she must be covering my ass. But that did remind me.

"I'll talk to Ray about work, but you know what I wanted to ask you? Was Gabin having an affair? Have you heard anything about it?"

There was a fairly long silence, then Elise released a breath. "I didn't want to say anything to you with everything going on, but there's been some serious shit going on at the restaurant."

"Like what?" Was it more than just Augustine's affair?

"Apparently Augustine had an affair with Trenton because Gabin has been sleeping with someone for, like, years. Auggie told Gab that the only reason he did any of it was to hurt him for the years of humiliation he caused him."

It was all so heartbreaking. Two men I looked up to, men I'd hoped to have a love like theirs, were a mess.

"Jesus. So what happened?" I asked wondering how all this affected the restaurant.

"Well, I heard yesterday that Gabin's lover was killed and it looks like this serial killer guy. Andy, it's such a mess. Auggie has been talking about closing down for a few week and taking Gabin away so they can try and rebuild from all this."

"Wait...." Gabin's lover was killed. "Who was Gabin's side piece?"

"Chad something, I don't really know more because Gabin was hysterical over it. He kept going on about how he had just seen him and now he was dead." I could hear Elise sniffle and it was no surprise, hearing the pain Gabin was in had affected her.

"And you didn't want to tell me because you thought I'd blame myself for this. Like this guy somehow did this because I work for Gabin or something?" Was that it?

"I didn't want to bother you. This killer is wiping out young gay men, Andy. The news started showing all the photos. They all resemble each other. Andy, you need to be careful."

"I am being careful Elise. Look, let me talk to Ray about work and let me know if Auggie really is going to close the restaurant for a while."

"Okay. Be safe. Talk to you soon."

After I disconnected my call I sat back and let all the information wash over me. It was horrible what happened to Gabin's lover. Terrible their marriage was in shambles, but I was certain neither Gabin nor Augustine had anything to do with the killings. Why would Gabin kill his lover? And why would Augustine do it after all these years? It didn't fit since all the guys had a message on their bodies for Ray. No, it wasn't Auggie's style. He didn't even like to watch the chef tenderize the meat in the kitchen.

Ray was still in his office on the phone, so I didn't want to disturb him. I'd tell him what I found out later. I wasn't sure if it would be of any help at all, but ruling people out was always a good thing.

My stomach rumbling made me realize it had been awhile since I ate. Ray would probably be starving so I rummaged through the fridge and cabinets to see what I could make. There was fresh ground beef in the fridge, an onion, some peppers, yeah, I could make some kick ass burgers. We could have chips on the side. Cooking took me away from my thoughts all the time.

I mixed all the ingredients in the bowl, but I wanted it to marinate for twenty minutes, so I sauntered into the living room and looked over the board Bradford, Ray, Richie, and I made with all the victims and information.

Epiphany was the hunting ground, that was glaringly obvious. We had two killers, one that grabbed, one that killed. One or both killers wanted Ray's attention. All the victims looked like this Mikey guy. Unless this phone call Ray was making led to the Holy Grail of information, something seriously drastic was going to have to be done. Every second these killers were on the streets another innocent life was brutally ripped room it.

The egg timer went off telling me the meat was marinated enough. I went back to the kitchen and began shaping the meat into patties. There were three kinds of cheese, so I shredded all three creating a mix. I reached over to wipe my hands and accidentally knocked the egg timer over making it crash to the floor breaking in two pieces.

"Dammit." I gathered it all up, but the mechanism wasn't clicking into place. "Crap I need the spring." Grabbing a flashlight above the fridge, I turned it on and looked under the oven. There it was in all its glory. Just unreachable. I had to ask myself, what would MacGyver do?

On Ray's fridge there were a bunch of flat magnets. I grabbed one, a piece of tape, and a straw creating a long handle. Slowly, I slipped it under the stove, excited when I saw the spring connect with the magnet.

"Yes!" I shouted in victory as I slid it out and grabbed the spring. "You thought you'd get away from me, Mr. Spring. Ha Ha. No one can resist a magnet..." It was like being hit with a ton of bricks.

"That's it," I whispered to myself. Quickly I put the egg timer back together. And while I knew Ray was still working, I also knew exactly how to lure out one of the killers. I may not get the one committing the actual crime, but if we got one, we'd likely get the other.

Without knocking, I opened Ray's office door. "I got it! Use me," I shouted at Ray who jumped and almost dropped the phone.

"Hold on," he said to whoever he was talking to. "Use you, Andy, what are you talking about?"

"Epiphany. Use me as bait. He won't be able to resist grabbing me."

"Let me call you back," Ray said and when he put his phone down, his expression didn't show he was excited.

"It's brilliant, Ray. You'll be there, you won't let anyone hurt me. I'm sure Bradford will help. He won't use one of his guys, but the more of us there, the less chance of anything going wrong."

Ray pinched the bridge of his nose. "Look, Andy, I get it. You want this to be over but risking you is a bad idea. Not to mention, what makes you think he won't see this as a trap?"

He had a point. I wasn't the detective type. Sure, I saw a lot of shows but....

"You're right, but what if there's a fake arrest? Make Green arrest someone, maybe they'll get angry or sloppy. Seeing me will be too irresistible to them." I didn't know why or how I became so brave. Honestly, the thought of going there to bait a mass murderer had me practically pissing my pants.

"It's not a bad idea, Andy. I need to talk to Bradford and everyone in the morning." He sniffed the air. "Are you cooking something?"

"Yeah, burgers. Okay, Ray, we eat and sleep, but you have to consider this as an option. They can't be out there forever killing people. No one has come up with a better idea or anything yet."

"Let's just eat. I learned a lot tonight."

I wanted to ask Ray a million questions, but his body was slumped in exhaustion and the circles under his eyes got darker every day. When Bradford and everyone was here tomorrow I'd toss out my idea with everyone else's and see if I had more allies in what I wanted to do.

22

RAY

As soon as Richie showed up, I'd left the house. We hadn't had the talk Andy wanted to the night before, but I'd wanted to get my head straight before I tried to explain everything. Andy had argued, wanting to come with me today, but it was just a few errands and a stop to pick up the information I'd put in a request for. Unfortunately, the head of the squad had retired a few months before.

I stared across a desk littered with empty, crushed paper coffee cups. The detective in the cheap suit and greasy combover was trying to bust my balls about chain of command. I never thought I'd throw out Green's name as a backup. He had told me whatever I needed, and I didn't know how important these files were, but my gut said I had to look at them.

Finally, the files were given to me after a big show of signing a bullshit form. I barely made it into the hallway of the basement of the precinct where Cold Case was located before I dropped the file box on a chair. According to the search parameters, a list of fifty cases came up. I was sure a serial murderer with that many kills would've come under scrutiny, but I had to go through each one. I didn't know how I felt about this leading back to Mikey, and possibly Finn.

I respected Finn, even as a criminal he had a code about what he would and wouldn't allow.

As I thumbed through the files in the box the beat of my heart picked up, and I could hear it echoing in my ears. The thrill of the hunt was back. That adrenaline rush I lived with for years. I couldn't deny that I was addicted to it, and this aspect of my work is what I'd missed the most.

Even as I felt myself succumb to the old spell there was one thing troubling me. I wasn't happy about the plan Andy came up with, but I couldn't disagree with the validity of it. Chasing shadows would only get us so far. We needed something bold that would draw the deadly partners out of the dark. The disorder of their new pattern proved they were on the edge, but I still didn't understand what that had to do with me.

Yeah, I had enemies, no cop made it through their career without collecting a few. I just wasn't all that comfortable with setting Andy up as bait. He wasn't a client. What he was, I wasn't quite sure. We'd become so mired in the case and the unpredictability of it that he and I hadn't discussed it.

I put the top back on the box so that I could get home to Andy. The sting had to be planned down to the smallest detail and because it was Andy, I was even more cautious. I'd made a few stops before I'd headed to the precinct. I wondered what he'd say about the vest I'd bought for him.

The one thing I didn't want to do was make Andy more fearful than he already was, and I needed to give him his life back. We hadn't discussed what would happen after the case was over, but I didn't want to let him go. The case, Andy, the what-ifs, all the unknowns were a fucked-up maelstrom of madness, and I felt like I was losing my mind. I returned to my car and stowed the box in the trunk.

Every decision I made as I drove back home was colored by what I thought was best for Andy. I pulled into the garage and hit the remote to close the door. I pushed a weary sigh through my compressed lips and got out of my car. I retrieved the box and bags, then headed inside.

When I walked through the back door, I smiled at the sight of Andy and the welcoming look on his beautiful face. I set everything on the table and leaned in to kiss him. His lips gave perfectly under mine.

"Hey, did you get everything you needed?" Andy asked as he wrapped his arms around my waist.

I rubbed his back and nodded. "I'm going to send Richie home. I know I kinda left you in the dark so we're going to talk."

"Okay."

I hated that I caused the nervousness in his voice I gave him one more kiss and then headed to the living room to find Richie staring at the boards.

"Hey, man."

"You know, all the shit I've done and seen…shit like this, I just can't get my head around it."

"Your humanity is showing."

"Fuck you, Clancy. You and your man good?" Richie asked as he stood.

"Yeah, tell Bradford that we'll get together tomorrow and get a plan in place."

I'd put off the talk with Bradford that morning only because I knew he would agree with Andy's idea. Yeah, I was more cautious than my former boss, but I'd lived under the weight of different rules since I became a cop. Sometimes I bent them, and I'd admit that. Yet I tried leave my old life behind.

"I know this…I know that kid in their means something to you, but we gotta do it. He ain't like us, he shouldn't live looking over his shoulder."

Richie slapped me on the back and then left without giving me a chance to respond. I'd always had a poker face. No one could ever tell what I was thinking. Richie had known me too long for secrets to exist between us.

"Richie looked funny when he left."

I turned at the sound of Andy's voice.

"I know you have a lot of questions, and I don't even know where to start."

"How about with who Mikey is?"

As Andy took a seat on the couch, I closed the distance to lower onto the coffee table. I curved my hands around the back of his calves.

I took a minute to gather my thoughts. "Just a small-town kid in a bad situation. Coming to the city to find a better life."

"Were you involved with him?"

"No. I just had a bit of a soft spot for him. Daniels liked to give me shit over the extra attention I paid some of the street kids. Said it looked bad with me being gay. I didn't announce that shit at work, but I sure as fuck didn't hide it. That's not important now.

"Mikey eventually got off the street and joined a service. It was safer for everyone, or so he'd assured me. And like I said, Mikey called me when a date went wrong. It took some doing but I got him to file a report, but after that I sent him home. I wanted so much to close that case."

"Ray, I'm sure you did everything you could. But why—"

He paused like he was trying to figure out how to phrase the question, but I sensed what he wanted to know.

"Most serials escalate over time, and Mikey was pretty carved up, but he survived. I think Mikey was the first, or at least an early victim. Our killer hadn't reached the point where he got off on the kill yet. Side by side, these kids could be siblings. When I called the Cold Case squad I asked them to look for cases that fit Mikey's and the current ones. I need to know when he'd escalated from torture to murder. The kids that he's picking, they're street smart and know how to handle their own."

"What would any of this have to do with you?"

"I don't know, baby, I really don't. I picked up all the files and I'm going to go through them, see how many of them have me as the lead. In no way can I figure out how someone could hate me so much they'd take it out on innocents. And it's fucking killing me."

I lowered my chin to my chest and inhaled deeply, exhaling slowly as I tried to calm myself. The guilt was too much, and I didn't know what to do with it. All I could do was find these fuckers and get them off the streets.

"This isn't your fault."

I didn't look up and kept my gaze focused on Andy's lap. I tested the soft texture of his well-worn jeans under the rough pads of my fingers. I needed something to ground me and bring me back to the Ray I used to be—the one I understood.

"No matter how much I tell myself that, it doesn't bring those kids back."

"What about using me as bait?"

"Fuck, I don't want to do that. I promised to keep you safe and putting you in danger doesn't sit right with me. But the rational part of me knows that we have to do something big to draw them out."

"You'll be there to watch me; I trust you."

Andy sounded so sure of me, and I hoped I didn't fail him. His soft hands cupped my cheeks and gently forced me to look into his blue eyes.

"Ray, I trust you. We'll get through this and when it's all through, we can go back to life as normal. I need my life back. My job. My friends. I need to be normal again."

"I know, I know, I understand and there's nothing else I want for you, but—Andy..."

Everything I wanted to say sounded idiotic.

Andy bent over and rested his arms on my knees. "Just say it."

"When we find them, and I mean when, what happens with us? What the hell is going on?"

23

ANDY

The vulnerability in Ray's eyes, and the slight wobble to his words when he asked about our future almost took my breath away. Through the midst of murder, he was worried about us. Admittedly, the question bounced around my head just as much as I questioned whether I would or wouldn't die. I didn't want to say I didn't know because that wasn't true. I did know, I wanted to stay with Ray, try and make us work. The fact he wanted that, too, was obvious just by looking at him.

"My whole life men didn't look at me with desire just while filling my coffee cup. Sure, they wanted a fuck here and there, but in the end they were gone without a glance back." Ray winced at my matter of fact tone, but it was truly the life I'd lived.

"Until you, Ray, I never felt handsome, lusted after, hell, I never felt—if I'm being honest."

He took my hands in his, tenderly he placed kisses on my knuckles. "Andy, I'm sort of glad other men haven't swept you away, otherwise I wouldn't be here with you wondering if you liked me half as much as I like you."

His words filled me with so much warmth I practically

giggled. "What I want is to be with you, Ray. Long after this case is done, but only if that's what you want, too."

He tugged me to him and without hesitation pressed his lips to mine. I felt every emotion flow through me as our tongues tangled, his arms wrapped around me, and his moans vibrating into the lustful air. Want, protection, need. I could fall head over heels in love with Ray Clancy, and it didn't terrify me at all.

The amazing make-out session was interrupted by the buzz of Ray's phone in his pocket.

"Damn," he mumbled against my lips. "Hold that thought." His expression was almost relaxed, I loved the carefree smile he gave me as he said hello to the caller.

Watching his happiness morph into anger and sadness was not something I wanted for this moment.

"I see. So we have no idea where he is or how to get a hold of him. Do we even know if he's still alive?" Ray spoke urgently to the caller. "Okay, you'll stay on it? Great. Thanks."

"Who was that?" I asked as I gripped his shirt, desperate to hold on to the good moment.

"Bradford." With a sigh he broke our embrace and relaxed in the chair. "Because Mikey was alive we thought he'd may be able to give us something on the person who attacked him. At the time he said it was fuzzy but something about it told me he knew. With all these killings and the similarities to the victims we, meaning Bradford and me, thought Mikey would see the situation as dire and talk."

This was great news. "What a great idea, Ray." I sat beside him desperate to understand why he wasn't happy, too.

"Bradford hired people to hunt him down. Went all the way to his hometown. According to his sister, she hasn't seen Mikey since the day he left years ago."

"He never went home?" I swore the bus ticket was to his house, at least that's what Ray had said.

"He was supposed to. Mikey didn't talk a lot about his home life, but I got the impression it wasn't all bad, just poor. I don't know what Mikey was thinking that day the bus drove away, but I guess it was to disappear."

"So, he's in the wind? Will Bradford keep looking?"

He nodded. "Yeah, but time isn't on our side, Andy."

I knew Ray was right. Every night was a gamble with this killer. More lives lost for a purpose no one understood. A killer with a vendetta. Was it jealousy, anger, or revenge? No one knew, and it was clear by the look on Ray's face he was feeling the suffocating desperation.

"Ray," I whispered. "You have to let me help. You have to let me at least try to lure them out."

"I hate it, Andy, so much can go wrong." The strain this whole situation had put on Ray was showing on his rugged face. From the dark circles, furrowed brow, and downturned mouth, it was obvious he despised this idea.

"Hey." I inched closer, gently cradled his scruffy cheek and lifted his head so his eyes met mine. "I was so scared that night in my apartment, and as I ran down the street, even on Elise's couch safe and warm I wondered when he'd find me. The hours felt like days and I had no idea what I was going to do. I thought I was going to be afraid until eventually I was killed. Then I met you. Yeah, I'm still scared, but for the first time I feel brave. I know nothing is going to happen to me because you won't let it."

He brushed his lips against my palm sending a shiver up my arm. "I've seen so much in my line of work, Andy, so so much." When he squeezed his eyes shut I wanted to straddle his lap and kiss his pain away. His next words stopped me. "I can't promise nothing bad will happen, but I can promise I'll die trying to save you."

I couldn't stop myself as I slid over his lap and kissed him breathless. With my mouth I tried to take away all his darkness.

His worry, his pain, his hate. I licked away the bad and tried to push all the good into him. When he wrapped his arms around my waist and pulled me closer, I wanted to laugh at the tiny victory.

"Andy," he spoke against my lips.

"Ray, god."

He pushed his hands under my shirt and gently scraped my flesh eliciting a throaty moan. Everything about Ray did it for me, from his sexy smile to his brilliant mind. What left me breathless was that he wanted me. I was done questioning it I was ready to jump head first into this and hope we both made it through these killers' psychotic games.

That night Ray ravished my entire body. I never felt more cherished than I did as Ray kissed, licked, and sucked every inch of my skin. His moans mingled with mine, and when we came together, I wanted to weep from the emotion bubbling inside me. I wanted a whole life with Ray, and I was going to fight to make that happen.

My sleep was riddled with nightmares. It started with Ray kissing me before going into the club and me suddenly getting lost in a maze of people. Hands grabbed my arms, screams broke out. Fire, fear, and shouts as flames engulfed Epiphany. With the chaos dancing around me I felt the hairs on the back of my neck stand on end… and then silence.

People struggling to breathe, the overwhelming sadness strangled me, and then I heard him. The voice from the phone. "I want to play, Andy."

I shot up from the bed gasping for air. I was soaked with sweat and tears poured from my eyes. I'd never felt so deeply in a dream.

"Andy?" Ray's sleepy voice pulled me from the depths of my fear. "What is it?"

I had to think fast, I couldn't have Ray know the terror that invaded my dreams. He'd never let me go to Epiphany.

"Nothing. I felt something on my leg. A fucking spider. Scared the shit out of me." I chuckled nervously. "Stupid I know."

Ray took my hand and pulled me close, wrapping me safely in his arms. "Creepy fuckers," he laughed, and I wanted so much to join him.

"Yeah."

I waited until Ray's breathing evened out and his grip loosened before slipping out of bed. Sleep wasn't happening now. Not after that.

It was only three in the morning, but my day was beginning. Today Ray was going to tell Bradford my plan and things would start moving.

I started a pot of coffee, took one of Ray's pads, and spent the next few hours while Ray slept writing everything I wanted Ray to know about me, him, and us.

If this plan went tits up, one day he'd find this and know that even though I wasn't there, I'd felt loved once, and he would know he was loved in return.

24

RAY

The circles under Andy's eyes were starting to worry me, and I didn't know how to put him at ease. He'd awakened me with his nightmares the last couple weeks, and I let him lie to me when he tried to play it off. I knew the only thing I could do was make sure Andy was safe and that meant taking on what had turned into my greatest fear—putting him in danger. I didn't give a fuck how many of Bradford's men would have our backs or the cops that would litter the crowd of Epiphany. It would only take one stupid slip up for everything to go nuclear. Although, their plan couldn't get any more perfect.

"So, how's this going to work again?" Andy asked as he went through the shopping bags I'd just placed there. "You all still leaving the cops in the dark about the backup team?"

He hadn't had clothes appropriate for going to a club, so I'd taken him shopping. I'd hated every fucking minute of it, and I put him in charge of helping me blend. I was more Jazz club or pub for a pint than some nightclub where everyone would probably be half my age. I leaned back against the headboard and just watched him.

As much as I was worried about him, I knew I was doing

everything in my power to make sure our operation went down without issues. That didn't mean there wasn't the possibility of fuck ups. I was more determined than before. After we'd had the talk about what would happen between us after they took down the killer and his partner, I was excited at the chance of keeping him and trying to have a normal relationship when he was safe.

"Bradford and his boy will be there to point out the man he'd seen with the other victims. And his guys will be there for some extra eyes. Bradford will contact me through my earpiece as soon as the partner shows."

The cops were still clueless about Bradford's involvement, or at least I thought they were. If they weren't then I was surprised by the absence of Green's bitching.

"Do you think it'll be that easy?"

"I don't know, I'm...hopeful."

"Where's the pessimist that I know and adore?"

"He's still very much there, I promise."

"What's Green going to think when he learns that you have criminals running backup?"

"They're just...misunderstood, there's no evidence." I chuckled at the playful roll of his eyes. "But in all seriousness, I don't trust Green and his team to care about more than taking down a killer."

"You don't think they'll have my safety in mind?" he asked as he glanced at me as he hung up a few shirts.

I shifted and crossed my ankles. "I'm not taking the chance. Come here." I patted my thighs and smiled as he approached, when he straddled my legs I wrapped my arms around him. "I promise I won't take my eyes off you for a second." I flexed to tug him closer and my man draped his arms over my shoulders.

"I trust you, I wouldn't even think about doing this if I didn't."

I leaned in to kiss the sexy tilt of his smile and deepened the kiss but refused to let it get out of hand. I wanted to make sure he was prepared for every step. Moments like this I could pretend that we were any other couple. I wanted to wake up one morning without the specters of killers hanging over our heads.

"I just want you safe, baby, and I'll do whatever I have to do."

"Don't put yourself in danger."

The worry in his voice almost made me lie, but I couldn't do that to him. It wasn't in me to provide false hope that I wouldn't get hurt.

"I can't make a promise like that. All I can tell you is I'll have my vest on and men I trust at my back."

I knew he wasn't satisfied with my answer.

"Baby, please listen to me."

I waited for him to raise his gaze from where it rested on my chest. He was nervously rubbing the sides of my t-shirt between his slender fingers. It took a few minutes, but finally he listened and turned his worried and slightly teary eyes up to me. I brought my hands to his cheeks and traced the lush curve of his lower lip with my thumbs.

"I'll do everything within my power to make sure we're both in one piece. I just can't lie. Honesty is important to me, and I need you to go into this with your eyes open and prepared for whatever."

"I get it, Ray, I really do, but...I just see the potential for more and I'm not ready to lose it."

I laughed when Andy squeaked as I rolled until I was on top and resting heavy in the cradle of his thighs. I awkwardly stripped Andy's shirt over his head one-handed. While I gently kissed him, I let my left hand roam over the silky smooth skin of his chest and stomach. I groaned as his hands slipped under my shirt and tweaked the hair on my stomach, then chest.

"We won't."

Whatever serious conversation we were going to have ended

as I teased his tongue with mine and we quickly stripped. As I slid balls deep I savored every sound he gave me, and I groaned as his nails dug into back. My pace increased as I pushed him toward release. I wanted his ecstasy before I took mine. His hole clamped down on my dick and his release painted our bellies. When I took his mouth roughly, I emptied into the latex and pumped my hips shallowly until my muscles relaxed. I collapsed on him and kissed him between labored breaths.

I looked forward to a life with him, and I wouldn't let a killer and his psycho partner fuck that up.

THREE NIGHTS HAD PASSED, AND MY FRUSTRATION GREW, I WAS living with a horrid techno beat repeating in my head even after we left Epiphany every night. I had to believe our plan would work. Although, we were on night four and still no takers, well, at least none that were our targets. I wasn't the jealous sort, or at least I hadn't previously felt that particular emotion. Every man who approached Andy caused me to growl from my secluded corner where I had a perfect view of him.

"Man, you're gonna have to relax," Richie warned, then took a draw off his beer. "That kid doesn't see anyone but you."

"I trust him," I protested. It never occurred to me that he would take any of the offers seriously.

Even the loud music didn't cover the man's snort that came through the earpiece. Okay, I wasn't hiding it well, and Andy had called me on it after the first night. I'd taken him home and fucked him against the wall as soon as we'd entered the kitchen. It was a bullshit alpha move and I wasn't proud of my actions.

"I didn't say you didn't."

I needed to change the subject, so I asked the first thing that popped into my head. "Is our plan going tits up?"

"We didn't expect instant gratification. Maybe they wised up after hitting too many back to back."

"It's another change in M.O. and I'm not comfortable with it."

Their targets had gone into a frenzy a month ago, kills barely days apart and now, they were coming up on two weeks without another body turning up. That wasn't something I would complain about, but I also knew that we needed another body, or at least for them to fuck up. I hated that another victim needed to surface, but it was the twisted nature of the game. Without forensics or at least a reliable witness ID, we were at a stalemate.

As much as I loved spending time with Andy and having him in my house, I needed to make him safe so we didn't have this dark cloud over us.

"Heads up gentleman, we have a major issue," Bradford's voice sounded in my ear.

"What's up?"

"We've spotted the supposed partner."

Before I could ask, I frowned as Benji, Finn's son, approached Andy. He pushed in close and crowded him, causing his man to flinch at whatever Benji whispered in his ear. I was off the stool and halfway to the two men with Richie at my six. Then things started to click, and I was sickened by the implications. I'd put Andy in danger without knowing it when I took him to Benji for help with tracking the phone.

I was only feet away from them when all hell broke loose. The deafening sound of fire alarms and the strobing of lights disoriented me, and I cursed as I lost sight of them. The sprinkler system rained down on us increasing the mob mentality of the crowd. I pushed bodies out of the way as hysteria took over and everyone panicked.

"Take Mac now," Bradford's order was growled.

I broke through the wall of fleeing bodies and Andy and Benji were gone. I turned in a circle and saw Andy's ashen face, saw his mouth form my name in a scream drowned out by sirens. I barely saw Bradford's men barreling through the crowd, but hundreds of people were blocking them.

My heart was in my throat as Richie and I combined our strength to tackle our way through. I could feel the cool air coming through the opened clubbed doors, but I no longer saw my targets. It seemed as if hours had passed before we reached the sidewalk where chaos reigned.

"Where the fuck are they," I yelled in an enraged voice as Bradford appeared on my other side while Richie stepped up.

I heard cops yelling freeze and turned to find them drawing down on Benji who was knelt on the sidewalk with a smile on his face. He looked as if he didn't have a care in the world.

I ran toward Benji and leaned down to grab the front of his t-shirt. "Where the fuck is he?" I moved in close and crouched down. "You don't want to fuck with me, where's Andy and your partner?"

"Detective, did you lose something?"

As I was about to throw a punch, Bradford's caught my arm in the crook of his elbow.

"Ray, if he's out cold we get no information. Get your shit together. Your boy is all that matters, you got me?"

The way the man dropped his smooth, posh vocabulary pulled me back from the edge.

"Clancy," Green called my name.

I tore my gaze away from Benji and found Green holding a laptop inside a bag. A piece of paper taped to the lid with my name and *watch me* written in thick block letters. I surged to my feet and jerked the computer from his hands. I tore off the plastic and opened it as I set it down on the trunk of a nearby car.

I cursed loudly as I waited for it to boot up, and in the middle of the screen was a folder simply labeled *Play*. I clicked on it and everything else faded away except for the fear that an unknown killer had Andy. They were currently on the way to some location and I had no idea where.

The video player loaded and my brain expected to see Finn, but who I saw shocked me more than anything: my ex-partner Daniels.

"Well, hello, Ray." The man's calmness terrified me. "I knew you'd come back to me, but I must say, you played so hard to get. If you're watching this, then I know you're aware that I have your little whore."

I clenched my back teeth and spread my hands on the cool metal beside the laptop.

"You really should have better taste than these…boys. First Mikey, but I took care of him even after you tried to send him away. I saw the way you looked at me, but you cheapened yourself with all those pretty whores. Every one of their deaths is your fault."

I sensed when my friends crowded at my sides, and I only looked away long enough to take in the crowd forming behind me.

"Green's boy was a bonus. The way he allowed you to lose your job, he deserved to be punished."

Green's gasp made me take in the way all the blood drained from the man's face.

"Benji will let you know how this is going to play out. Follow his rules and your whore will probably survive. He just might not be as pretty as when you lost him."

The video ended and I turned on Benji.

"What the fuck does he want?"

"Not that easy, Detective."

"Ray, I'm gonna call Finn, we might need him."

I didn't answer Richie. All I could think were worst case scenarios and that even now, Andy could be the victim of the same as all those other young men. All the crime scene photos played out in my head, including the even modulation of Donnelly's voice during the autopsies. I was barely keeping it together as I realized the game Daniels was playing was far from over.

"Get him to the station now," Green ordered and then turned to me. "Clancy, you got this shit? I don't want another crime scene, do you understand me?"

All I could do was nod, and then we were all on the way to the station. Benji was shoved into the back of a black and white, and I was in the back of Bradford's limo.

"If anything happens to Andy—"

"There will be nothing left of Daniels, I don't care how far he tries to run." His voice cold as he made me the promise.

I took a sliver of comfort that my oldest friend would have my back. I wouldn't let all my hope slip away. Daniels wanted something from me, wanted me, and he needed Andy for that. That meant my man would be alive for now, but for how long?

25

ANDY

My entire body felt like it was being held down with bricks. My head pounded, and while I'd never done drugs in my life, I had a sneaking suspicion I was under the influence of something by the way my heart was racing and the double vision. I tried moving, but it was like my brain was unplugged from the rest of my body.

"Oh, Mr. Shay, good to see you're awake." I'd heard that voice before, outside the club. "Don't try and move, it would be pointless."

I opened my mouth to speak, but I couldn't. What the hell was wrong with me?

"You're probably a little disoriented, I imagine it's a terrifying feeling." The man chuckled. "Let me position you better so you're not on your stomach and can look at me. Not making eye contact is so rude, isn't it?" He spoke like he was sorry for inconveniencing me, but at the same time, was going to continue to do so.

Suddenly my body was hoisted up. While I wasn't a large man, I knew it was dead weight so this guy was obviously in good form, which only scared me more. Where was Ray?

My head fell forward so that all I could see was the man's shoes. The sound of plastic and the scraping of a chair echoed. The smell was oddly familiar, and I was able to move my eyes. The floor was covered in broken linoleum and gray concrete underneath. Again, the familiarity niggled at my mind.

My body was dragged until I was laying on what looked like a blue tarp. It was in that moment I realized where I was, seeing the white fairy lights above my head and the man-made tropical leaves in Lily's Oasis. The one place I found peace.

"Hey," the guy said snapping in front of my face. "I really love what you did here. Looks so peaceful. I can see why you'd bring Ray and want to make it special."

I followed the sound of his voice with my gaze. Did I know him? I remembered Benji and how when I saw him approach at Epiphany I wanted to tell him to go away, I didn't want him to blow my cover.

But he smiled at me like he knew. And it was confirmed when he leaned down and whispered words into my ear that made cold fear race through my body. "It seems you've been waiting for me," Benji had whispered. "I had to get things set up so Ray, Bradford, and all the lingering cops wouldn't follow us. Now, it's about to get loud and wet, but there's someone I need to take you to. So, don't make a fuss."

Benji, Finn's son? I never saw it coming. I knew he worked with his father, but it never crossed my mind Finn would be some sadistic fuck. But the man I was with now was definitely not Finn.

In the brief moment I saw Ray's face through the crowd I shouted his name even though I knew he saw me, it was all I could do. It was pure madness and I was yanked away and tossed in a car.

Then a voice said, "Time to go to sleep." A prick in the neck and now I was at my oasis, with a serial killer, no Ray, and the feeling of utter loss.

"Allow me to introduce myself." The man crouched in front of me. "My mom liked to call me Charlie, but I hated that. Then in school they called me Charles. I equally hated that. My middle name Barron was just as bad. So, I decided to just use C.B., and then of course, my last name Daniels." He held his hand out to me and chuckled. "Right, no handshake."

C.B. Daniels. Now that was a name I knew. Ray's ex-partner. Richie was right to watch him. We should've paid more attention.

"I don't know if Ray will find us here, but I think we have some time to play before he does." His smile was blinding and not in the way that was charming. It was slimy, bright white, fake. He was an average looking man with brown dull hair, brown eyes, and a medium build. Absolutely nothing special. No wonder no one could remember seeing him. There was nothing that stood out about him.

I watched helplessly as he brought over the black doctor's bag I remembered seeing when I walked in on him carving up Francis.

"The first night Benji told me he saw you at Epiphany I knew something was up," he huffed as he opened the bag. "I had Benji set up a system to rig the place and I watched you." The sudden expression of disgust on his face and the slam of the bag would have made me jolt away if I could. "You were baiting me with your whorish ways. I bet Ray thought you were new to it all, but I know your type. Any port in a storm." His sinister eyes met mine and he held up a scalpel. "Any dick too."

No. That was so far beyond who I was. And if the fact this guy didn't slice up his victims as they lay helpless made him crazy, his delusions sure did.

"I'm sure if you could talk you'd tell me what I've heard

many times before, that you aren't a slut. That you don't open your legs for anyone at all." He scoffed as I watched him sanitize the scalpel. Odd thing to do, but this whole situation was my worst nightmare.

"I wanted to get to you for a while now. At first it was when you walked in on me with your roommate. That was a huge shock. It's not easy for something like that to get past me." He stared into the shiny weapon. "Then you went to Ray, and that was when I knew you had to go."

He placed the scalpel on a crisp white sheet beside the chair. I followed as much as I could, but not being able to move my head left me limited.

"You were seducing him at every chance. Convincing him you loved him I bet." He shook his head, once again disgust was directed at me. "Pretty boys. You flutter your eyes and make men swoon at your feet. It's pathetic." He gripped my hair and pulled my head back, the pain was quick, fierce and my inability to scream explained exactly why none of his victims could call for help.

"Ray always wanted me, always," he shouted in my face, spittle spraying over me. "But boys like you always kept pulling him away. I knew I was going to have to give fate a push and begin ridding the world of all of you one at a time. I knew Ray would finally see me as I saw him without the distraction of all you little sluts."

When he released my head, it fell forward. I wanted so badly to scream, fight back, tell Daniels he was a lunatic, if for no other reason than to get the last word.

I didn't want to die, but more, I didn't want Ray to die. I knew he'd figure it out, he was brilliant. I knew Daniels and Benji would pay. But my heart ached because I'd never get my forever with Ray. I'd never see his smile, hear his muffled irritation when I organized or cleaned something in his house. I'd never do all the things I'd hoped to do.

"Ray needs to see how ugly you really are inside. I will take away all the things you whores seduce men with. Your eyes, your skin, your little pathetic dicks."

C.B. gripped my chin painfully forcing eye contact. "We should begin. This will hurt a lot I'm sure. But in the end, realize what you are and that you deserve every second of it." He narrowed his eyes. "You could have avoided all this, Andy, if you never called Ray. Let that fester in your head while I dismantle your body a piece at a time."

He reached for a pair of scissors. "First, let's take off your hooker gear. Look at your disgusting body." He cut and tore at the fabric. I felt every piece being removed. The chilly air against my sweat soaked skin covered my flesh in goosebumps. He maneuvered my body until every stitch was gone and I sat there naked, paralyzed, and helpless.

"There." He was slightly out of breath. "I just don't see what Ray sees in you pretty boys. Pasty skin, lanky, it's gross."

This was nothing I didn't hear my whole life and normally it would hit me hard, but his words didn't faze me one bit. Ray made me feel like I was the most gorgeous person in the world. And if I was to die here today, I'd die knowing that I was loved and cherished.

"Let's begin," he said.

I said a silent prayer to who I didn't know. I wasn't sure if there was a God or a giant bug in the sky, but I didn't want to die. I didn't want to hurt, and I didn't want Ray to find me mutilated like I did Francis. Right as Daniels was about to slice something across my chest, a sound came out of my mouth.

"What?" He halted, and I tried to take advantage.

"Th... Thank. Thank you."

He crouched down again, his face before me. "How'd you speak? I gave you enough to paralyze a horse."

"Thank you." I spoke more clearly that time.

"Thank you?"

"For freeing me." Yeah, two can play the crazy game.

"Freeing you?" I could tell he was completely bewildered.

"Yes. I… wanted to." I swallowed. My voice felt like sandpaper. "I wanted to get away, from Ray."

C.B.'s laughter was maniacal. "You expect me to believe that?"

I tried nodding, but that was still a no go. "Yes. He just…. All I ever heard about was this partner of his. The one… the one who got away."

The brief softening of his eyes told me that was something he longed to hear.

"Me?" Daniels voice cracked.

"Unless he had another partner."

I knew Ray had never worked with anyone else, and I knew Daniels was aware of that fact, too. I could only hope that he didn't see past my ruse and I could buy Ray time. Time to find me. I only hoped he remembered this place and that Benji was spilling everything.

26

RAY

They were wasting fucking time and that smug fuck was just sitting there like he had all the time in the world. He kept asking the time every five minutes. I stared through the two-way mirror into the interrogation room. It took everything in me to keep my hands from shaking. I needed to get my shit together or I wasn't going to be of any use to Andy.

Just the thought of him brought the panic back, reminding me how helpless I was. Yeah, I had a soft spot for the kids that drew the short straw in life. I never once thought I'd be punished for it. All those fucking kids dead because of me. Now, the first man I cared for was going to pay for some delusional man's assumptions.

How many had Daniels killed because he thought I belonged to him?

"Ray, don't do it. Don't let him in your head."

"Too late. He's been there for months."

I turned my head to look at Bradford. I thought we'd agreed that he would get away from the precinct and wait for my call. When Andy had quipped about Bradford's badge envy, it wasn't that much of a joke. He easily stepped inside and closed the door, for being in a station of cops that looked at him as a career arrest the man was way too fucking calm.

"Thinking about a career change?"

"No, the coffee is terrible."

I couldn't help my grin at his exaggerated shudder. The man knew me better than anyone. He was there from my first stolen car and beatdown to extract a debt.

"What if I can't keep it together? All I want to do is rip the fucker's throat out."

"You'll keep it together because your boy needs you."

"Andy is far from a boy."

"Semantics, my old friend. You lived for this job and took pride in it, man, but deep down you're one of us. And we know how to handle all those pesky problems."

Bradford's elegant façade crumbled and the monster I knew peeked through. I'd witnessed his cruelty, and no matter how much of a respectful businessman he came across as, he was still that enforcer his old man groomed him to be.

"Where's Richie?"

"He and our men are waiting for my call. We can be on the move in minutes."

"If something happens to me, I need you to make it right."

"Nothing is going to happen to you. We take care of our own.

"He dies, Bradford."

"In the most horrible ways we can imagine."

I nodded in silent agreement and took a deep breath. I'd ordered Green to stay out of the interrogation room. I knew how the Mac family worked, but nothing about Benji's actions aligned with Finn.

"Did you talk to Finn?"

"Talk is not quite the word I'd use. He wanted Benji turned over to him."

"He's a fucking idiot if he thinks I'm gonna let that happen."

"Finn wants to handle...in house."

The lure of the temptation scared me. Yet I knew that it wouldn't get us the information we needed. My body stiffened as Benji stood and walked toward the glass. As Benji knocked on the glass, I raised my hand to turn on the intercom.

"Clancy, ya might want to bring my laptop."

I was in movement before the last word was out of his mouth and grabbed the computer from a table at the back of the room. When I entered the squad room, I found cops watching me impatiently, but they were feeling the pressure for different reasons. I pulled the calm around me and I glanced at Bradford to find him tapping his earpiece, I was still wearing mine as well. I quickly turned mine on and he disappeared as I entered the room.

Whatever it took, I'd get Andy back and I'd do it my way.

I squared my shoulders and motioned for Benji to sit back down. I laid the laptop on the table and he was already in motion. Opening the lid and starting to tap away at the keys.

"Finally, ready to talk, huh?"

"You old-timers are so fucking easy. Daniels thought he had me wrapped around his little finger. He was disgusting the way he grunted away and wanted to pretend I was you. You made quite the impression on your ex-partner."

Bile burned at the back of my throat. The rational part of me knew I hadn't done anything to lead the fucker on, but—I shoved all of that away. I didn't have time for reflection. Daniels needed me to play out his fucked up little plan, but how long would he wait before he tried to take Andy out? As we spoke, he could have started his ritual.

"What the fuck does he want?"

I rested my shoulders back against the wall beside the door, and as casually as possible, shoved my hands into my jean's pockets. It was more for my safety than his. I wanted to grab the front of his t-shirt and throw him around the room until he gave me what I needed. No one would attempt to stop me. I knew there was probably a crowd growing on the other side of the mirror.

"What do you think the crazy fucker wants? You."

"How did you hook up with him?"

He snorted and smirked. "Closeted men are so manipulatable. Scared shitless someone will learn that deep-dark secret that they like a dick up their asses or they like to gag on a cock or two. He busted me and my old man was done with my shit. I gave him a piece of ass to let me go. Then the situation changed. He framed you for the bribe hoping to come in and save you."

I forced my hands not to curl into fists in the confines of my pockets at finding out that not only had Daniels taken Andy, but my badge as well. "Save me?"

"Come up with the evidence that I would supply after the job I did to frame you. Then you took the deal before he could sweep in like your knight in shining armor."

"I'm not getting this bullshit."

"All this shit," He waved his arms around the room. "He was supposed to help me get rid of dear old dad, and I'd help him take out all those pretty boys at Epiphany. He had a very long list of twinks you mighta flirted with or fucked since the day he met you, but when you left Sex Crimes and transferred to homicide, you broke his poor little heart."

He talked too easily about taking out Finn, and from what I knew, his old man doted on him. Had never told him no once in his life.

"Why would you want to take out Finn?"

"Easy, I was done following orders. Finn's a relic. Unable to move forward with the times. Getting…soft."

"What game is Daniels playing?" I asked.

"Quite simple, Clancy, look." He spun the laptop around.

The air froze in my lungs as I saw Andy under a halo of light and tied naked to a chair. He looked to be struggling with keeping his head up. I tried to keep my head in the game and searched the surroundings in the frame. Everything looked like hundreds of industrial spaces in New West. A timer counted down at the bottom of the screen. They had less than an hour to do whatever the hell Daniels wanted.

I wanted to refuse. I wanted to tell Benji and Daniels to fuck off, and make sure they rotted behind bars for the rest of their lives. Yet I was trapped, restrained by their rules. I removed my hands from my pockets and curled them into fists. I placed them on the table and rested my weight on them as I moved in closer to the screen.

"You have," he peeked at the screen, "fifty-six minutes to get to your pretty, little whore. I almost fucked up the plan just to get a taste of that sweet, tight ass. I did enjoy the perks of my role but had to forego with Andy. I bet that boy loves to be pounded, begs for it. He definitely sounded good screaming your name when I watched all those intimate moments. Your security system is a piece of shit."

Fuck rules, I swung before I fully thought it through and felt satisfaction when him and the chair hit the floor. Blood flowed from his nose.

"Where is that Clancy calm? I heard about you. Man, they still talk about how vicious you were. Obeyed without conscience. A sought-after enforcer. Do your fellow brothers in blue know all those nasty things you did before you pinned on that hunk of metal?"

I didn't have the time or inclination to justify my choices in life. He was wasting my and Andy's time. "What the fuck does Daniels want?"

He eased up from the floor and fixed his chair. All I could do was stare as the seconds ticked down.

"You have fifteen minutes to arrange for a car to be waiting outside. You and I will get into the car, once inside I will relay directions, and if at any point I think we're being followed, I'll clam up and your boy dies. Tick-Tock, Clancy, Andy's running out of time."

I stormed from the room just as Green stepped out of the observation room.

"You're not going alone, Clancy, I don't—"

"I don't give a fuck, have the car ready. Is there any way to trace the signal?"

"It's bouncing all over the fucking place, right now. It's looks like Daniels is in Belfast."

"Motherfucker! Get a car ready now. And if you fuck this up, I'll make you pay worse than I'm going to make Daniels suffer."

I headed for the nearest bathroom and slammed the door behind me. I turned to rest my forehead on the cool wood and tried to take deep, even breaths.

"Ray, you copy," Richie's voice pulled me back from my meltdown.

"Go ahead."

"We're in position and ready to move. We've got eyes everywhere. I'll give a description of the vehicle. Daniels and Benji won't know we're on your ass."

I confirmed and spent the next fifteen minutes arguing until Benji and I were alone in the car. I repeatedly checked the mirrors and the only familiar vehicle I saw was a motorcycle that disappeared and reappeared. He droned on, we took several lefts and rights as Benji studied the traffic behind us.

Thirty-seven minutes, the counter was moving too fast, and with each second that ticked off, the knot of fear in the middle of my chest threatened to suffocate me. I tried not to focus on anything other than his words and finally the turns ceased.

Something about the area we drove into caused a mixture of

rage and sickness. I remembered this route. Andy and I had driven it a short time ago. And the sloppiness of my own actions hit me hard.

"Seem familiar?"

I ignored his question as I pulled up behind the abandoned warehouse and noticed the door stood wide open. The click of the laptop lid was too loud and harsh; I was out of the car and scanning the area.

"Keep it together, Ray, we move on your word," said Bradford.

I hadn't expected him to run backup. As far as I knew he tried to stay out of the dirty work these days. I didn't answer him and jogged around the car to open the door, then dragged Benji out.

I reached for my weapon in the holster at my hip. Savored the familiar weight of it and the coolness of metal. I hooked the fingers of my free hand in the collar of his t-shirt and shoved him forward. Daniels might not want me dead, but that didn't mean I didn't want a shield in case. The trip inside was slow and every step carefully made.

No lights shone until suddenly the place lit up. I barely restrained myself from running forward at the sight in front of me. Andy was naked and his upper body marred by shallow lacerations. Sweat and blood made his skin shimmer under the lights.

"You made good time, Ray. Was he followed?"

"Not that I could tell, we made turns all over the fucking place. I won't say they won't show up eventually."

I pushed Benji and the man stumbled forward as I took my weapon in both hands. The almost invisible tremors in my hands threatened to give away my nerves.

"Andy," I called his name.

"Don't worry, he's...well, for now. I gave him a paralytic, but rest assured he felt every cut."

I kept them both in my sights as I carefully made my way to Andy. When I reached him, I dropped to one knee and raised my hand to stroke his cheek. His skin was cool to the touch

"Don't touch him!"

The hysterical edge to Daniels' tone warned me that the man barely held onto his sanity.

"Ray," Andy's broken voice urged me to look at him.

"Baby, I'm right here."

"I'm so sleepy," he slurred.

"Just hang on for me."

"Where's my payment, Daniels?" Benji demanded.

"It's right here."

The reverberation of a single shot echoed in the cavernous space, making the sound sharp and it zinged my eardrums. I jerked my gaze to find Benji with a hole between his eyes.

"I'm sorry you had to see that, Ray, but he ruined so many of my plans. Led around by his dick. No better than all the whores I killed."

Even if Daniels made it out of here tonight, he'd just sealed his fate. Traitor or not, Finn wouldn't let his son dying go without retribution.

I dug my knife out of my pocket and quickly cut the zip ties that secured Andy's wrists and ankles to the chair. He instantly collapsed against my side with his head on my shoulder. His breathing ragged where it fanned against my throat. He didn't wrap his arms around me or whisper my name again.

"Why? What the fuck were you thinking?" I demanded.

I eased Andy to the dirty floor, hating the necessity of it and reached for a sheet that was close by. I tucked it around him and straightened. Daniels looked older and as forgettable as I remembered. He looked like thousands of other men walking the city streets. He blended so easy for years, and worse, he hid under my nose the entire time we rode together.

He took a few steps forward.

"Don't fucking move," I ordered as I side-stepped, removing Andy from his line of sight.

"You don't have to pretend anymore, Ray. I knew you were the one for me the minute we met. It was fate, can't you see that?"

"You're fucking insane."

"No, please, don't deny it. I saw the way you looked at me. You loved me, but we don't have to act anymore."

He kept moving toward me, and I finally stopped in a position where Andy was out of the firing line. Daniels tapped the barrel of his Glock against his thigh in an agitated rhythm. As much as I wanted to call in backup, I wanted to know why more than anything. I felt as if I was drowning under the weight of guilt from Andy's suffering and all the boys killed in the name of Daniels' twisted love.

I knew I had to attract his anger, vest or not, that wouldn't stop a head shot. He had wicked aim and I knew he never missed. As long as Andy survived, I didn't care about me. Bradford would take care of him for me and avenge my death.

"I didn't look at you any way. I worked with you. We weren't even friends. Fucking you would've been the last thing—"

"Shut up! Is that...thing what you want. Some whore." His voice rose several octaves as he started to turn to Andy.

"Daniels," I spoke sharply and drew his attention back to me.

My chest began to heave as I tried to bring oxygen into my lungs as the panic threatened to make me lose it. He was ranting and the words ran together. He paced and swung his weapon wildly, and then rage turned to something else. Tears began to flow down his cheeks and his body seemed to deflate.

"I did all this for you, Ray, to prove to you that I could be what you wanted—needed."

In slow motion I watched his right arm move in tiny increments until the weapon was pointed directly at me. I stared down my barrel at him. It was a standoff and the moment of truth had arrived. Live or die, it would be decided in a single breath and gentle squeeze of a trigger.

"I never wanted you or anyone, not until a scared man asked me for help. You're never going to have me, Daniels."

I didn't focus on his face. I gazed into the blackness and took solace in the fact that if I died, he died, but Andy would go on to live a long life without looking over his shoulder. It was barely a microsecond, but I didn't miss the flex of his trigger finger. I slowly inhaled.

"If I can't have you, then..." He paused.

I exhaled and gently compressed the trigger. Two shots rang out and agony exploded along my left collarbone, I felt myself falling. I didn't know if he was dead or on his way to the Hell, but images of Andy and overwhelming pain took the last of my control. I shuddered upon dirty cement and I couldn't lift my head, but I searched for Andy. He was right where I'd left him with the sheet tucked around him.

The pounding of steps blended with the roaring of my heartbeat in my head.

"Officer down, get the paramedics now." A voice I felt I should recognize joined the pandemonium inside my head. My eyes rolled upward. All I could think was Andy was safe and I'd done my job. That's all that I'd wanted to do, but I mourned the fact I wouldn't be around to see him live out the rest of his life.

Someone was calling my name, and then nothing at all.

27

ANDY

Without opening my eyelids, I heard the chaos of the hospital. Nurses and doctors shouting out medicines and procedures. Words like lacerations, bleeding, and long words no average person could possibly know. I was afraid to open my eyes. Like if I did, reality would come crashing down on me.

Daniels almost bought my reverse psychology, but then like a twig snapping so did he, and he lashed out across my chest. With the paralytic in me, I couldn't move much and could only grunt. But the pain, it was searing. He laughed and called me a whore, slut, cheap. Over and over. The longer no one arrived the more hopeless I felt. But Ray was safe.... And then he wasn't.

Laying there on the disgusting warehouse floor watching as Daniels lost his mind even further while having a standoff with Ray was terrifying. I couldn't even help. I was only able to speak softly, every time I tried to scream it came out as a loud whisper. I felt each tear as it fell, and when Ray slumped to the floor, I almost wished Daniels had killed me too.

Then everything went into frantic chaos. Richie stood over

me wrapping the blanket around me. I heard paramedics argue with him when he lifted me.

Voices shouting, Bradford telling Richie to stay with me and that he would go with Ray. I wanted to run over and grab Ray and bring him back to me.

Richie didn't leave me. Not once. Much to the doctors' frustration. I had no idea how long I had been in the hospital, but the fact I could move my body was a relief. One doctor said that amount of the manmade paralytic was toxic, and the fact I was alive after that in itself was a miracle.

I dozed a lot and didn't want to hear the words that Ray was dead, so when people came into the room I pretended to be asleep.

"You suck at acting." The sound of Bradford's voice made me flinch and any hope of convincing him I was out cold went right out the window.

"Please just leave me alone, Bradford." I didn't want to talk to anyone, I wanted to wallow. For the first time I had been in love and loved back, and now it was over.

"I can't do that. I promised Ray I'd check up on you." Ray's name on his lips had me turn my head so fast the dull headache behind my eyes thumped.

"No, Bradford, you have no ties to me. I don't care if Ray asked you to watch over me with his last breath, I don't want...." The sobs wracked my body. It was painful everywhere, my skin, bones, heart, all of it.

"Hey," Bradford hushed me and in an uncharacteristic move, he tenderly scooped me up into a hug.

He sat there on my hospital bed with me on his lap and hushed me.

"Andy, you've got it all wrong."

I'd soaked Bradford's shirt and normally I'd feel like an ass for being so careless, but I just didn't care.

"What exactly do I have wrong, Bradford?" I was snappish and angry, but Bradford smiled. It was one of pure pleasure, and I wondered just how sick in the head this man was to be joyful at a time like this.

"Andy, Ray's not dead."

I wasn't sure if it was some cruel joke or I was hearing things wrong, so I asked him to repeat it.

"I said he's not dead. He's not going to be playing baseball any time soon, or much of anything until he's healed, but he's alive."

Realizing that Bradford was telling the truth had me leaping off his lap and, on very unsteady legs, darting out of the room.

"Andy," Bradford shouted at me. "Stop."

I had no idea where Ray was, and I was also feeling a very chilly breeze on my backside.

Suddenly a blanket was wrapped around me. "Come back to your room, I'll have a wheelchair brought to you and I'll take you to him. I promise."

I wanted to argue so badly, but exhaustion made that impossible.

I sat on the chair and watched as Bradford asked a nurse to please bring a wheelchair to the room. He sat on my now vacated bed, smiled, and told me what happened.

"Daniels did in fact shoot Ray and for a minute, I thought he was a goner. There was a lot of blood, and I won't lie and say it wasn't touch and go for a while there. But in the end, Ray was lucky. There's really no other way to describe it. We didn't consider Daniels would have armor piercing bullets, but we should have considering he was a cop and knew Ray or the others would be wearing a vest. Where he was shot there's a fifty-fifty chance of fatality. But he's too tough for that."

"He's alive? Where is he, what's happened? Why didn't anyone tell me?"

He nodded in understanding. "Ray broke his collarbone and he's had several surgeries already. You've been out for four days. I didn't want anyone telling you anything just in case something happened during one of the procedures." He chuckled. "It didn't help that every time someone came into the room you pretended to be sleeping beauty."

When the nurse arrived with the wheelchair Bradford helped me get situated, and he pushed me down the hallway.

"He's on the floor above you," he said as he rolled me into the elevator.

I didn't know why I felt nervous. It wasn't because I didn't know what Ray would look like, but I thought he was dead, and now he's alive and... The pull of the stitches over my chest made me gasp.

"Yeah, be careful. You have a lot of stitches. But there's creams that will help with scarring." I looked up at Bradford and he winked. "Besides scars are sexy."

On Ray, sure. I wasn't positive they'd look great on me.

We went down a long corridor, and when Bradford rolled me into Ray's room, I didn't hold back. I cried once more, this time in happiness.

Ray was grumbling to a nurse as she desperately tried to show Ray how the sling worked. At the sound of my crying, Ray turned his gorgeous eyes my way.

"Andy." He spoke my name almost reverently.

I didn't care what the doctors or nurses said. I jumped out of the wheel chair and into Ray's one open arm. I didn't want to hurt him, but it was like I couldn't get close enough.

"Oh, god, Ray, I thought I lost you."

He kissed my head as I pressed my lips against every available piece of him.

"No way." He paused my franticness and cupped my face in his hand. "I have too much to live for."

"I love you so much, Ray."

"Not even half as much as I love you."

I heard Bradford usher the nurse out of the room and the click of the door. But after that it was Ray's heartbeat, his kisses, and his smell that took over.

I WAS ABLE TO LEAVE THE HOSPITAL A FEW DAYS AFTER discovering Ray was in fact alive. It would be another week before the doctors discharged Ray, however. So I was able to get to the house and clean up. Bradford hired a maid service and a chef to get food ready for us because, he said, even though I was out of the hospital I had to take it easy.

Richie brought me to the hospital to get Ray, and the look of relief on his face as we drove away from there was almost comical.

"If I never go back to a hospital it'll be too soon," he said as he laced his fingers with mine in the back seat of Richie's car.

"Have you talked to Finn?" I asked in the silence of the car. Richie was looking at Ray in the mirror obviously waiting for his response.

"He visited me in my hospital room the other night." He flinched when Richie growled. "Yeah, and that right there is why I didn't want to say anything." He pointed at Richie, and while I didn't like Finn going to Ray with no backup, I trusted Ray's instincts. I never met Finn, knew only what I'd heard from Ray, the media, and anyone else who dared talk about the man. If Ray felt like Finn wasn't a threat, I wouldn't press the issue.

"What did he say?" I squeezed his hand in reassurance.

"He's mourning his son. He wants to be angry about what he did, but I think he's having a hard time reconciling it. Finn admitted Benji was always trying to push modern technology on him, but he never thought his own son would turn the direction he did." Ray shook his head. "He thanked me for killing Daniels, even though he wanted him to die by inches he considered it squared away."

"Does Finn have any more kids? What happens to him now?"

"From what I know of Finn, Benji was his only kid. He'll be up to his eyeballs in cops for a while. It's hard to convince a police force that you had nothing to do with it when your son was involved and you're a mob boss."

I knew that was true and I felt bad for Finn.

"Heard Green's wife filed for divorce." Richie chuckled from the driver's seat. "Taking him for all he's worth."

Now that was a man I didn't feel bad for at all. He deserved all that and more.

"Maybe he'll stop playing the closet game now." Ray lifted my hand to his lips. "It's dark in there."

When Richie dropped us off at Ray's, it was a relief when no bodyguards stayed. It was just Ray and me.

The house was quiet and when Ray yawned, I convinced him to go lay down.

"Nap with me?" He was a little pathetic with his droopy eyes and, yeah, that's a pout.

"Sure, and when you wake up, let's watch a cheesy horror move, eat a million carbs, and pass out as far away from reality as we can?"

He smiled and pressed his lips to mine.

"Perfect plan."

EPILOGUE

ANDY

Six Months Later

"Didn't you ever watch the Karate Kid?" I shouted up to Ray as he stood on a ladder in front of our house.

"Of course I did."

"Then wax on wax off, you keep painting like that and it's going to look like a Jackson Pollack painting." I chuckled when he grumbled something about being a slave driver.

My attention was pulled from Ray's delectable ass at the sound of the mailman. I walked to the mailbox and took the envelopes from him, shuffling through until I saw what I was waiting for.

"Ray!" I shouted, causing the bucket of paint to fall from the ladder and onto the lawn. "Sorry, but look." I waved the envelope.

"Is that?"

"Yes."

He rushed down the ladder and ran over to me. "Open it."

"I can't." Thrusting it at him, he rolled his eyes and tore it open. I watched his face as he read it.

"Well," he sighed, and the rejection flooded over me. "It

looks like come the fall you'll be attending New West College." He smiled brightly, and I smacked him on the chest.

"You jerk! You had me thinking I didn't get in. But I did." I wrapped my arms around his neck and kissed the breath out of him.

"You're going to be amazing, Andy."

"So are you Mr. Police liaison man thing."

Ray laughed and shook his head. "Thank god that's not my title. I'm helping out on a movie set. An expert in police procedure and crime."

"Mmhmm, and you're writing a book... hence the man-thingy thing."

"I'm not letting you use words anymore." He slapped my ass. "Let's go shower and get dressed. This is cause for celebration. Bradford asked just this morning if you heard, yet, so let's see if he's free and we can all go out to dinner."

"That would be perfect."

I ran inside with Ray close on my heels. I never laughed so much as I did these last six months. Ray woke up a dormant person in my heart. I was going to school to be a teacher. I wanted to help children. No more hours on the floor waiting on other people. I was so glad when Elise announced she was going to open her own trinket shop near her sister. Even though she never admitted it, I knew the murders here had tainted her from ever living in New West again.

Ray was a man who didn't know what he wanted to be until a feisty red head was relentless about him telling his story and using his knowledge. Ray always complained how TV shows got it wrong, as did the movies, so now that feisty red head was his agent. He was writing a book, helping on sets, and smiling a lot more.

Green of course begged him to stay on the force per the mayor's order, but Ray gave him the finger and told him to fuck off. He couldn't do it anymore, the people who were supposed to have his back above all others burned him and all trust was gone.

I officially moved in with Ray shortly after he was released from the hospital, and I only had one condition. Make this house a home.

I knew I wanted kids someday, and I knew Ray would be an outstanding father. I thought when I mentioned it to him one night that he'd run away screaming, but he just said he had never thought about that until now.

Our lives were good. More importantly they were safe. I stopped looking over my shoulder. Ray kept his gun in his safe more often than not, and we had friends.

Bradford visited more than I ever thought he would, and I suspected he was lonely. I tried setting him up once with this guy I knew, but it was the worst mistake ever, and Bradford made me promise to never do that again. A matchmaker I was not.

All my life I felt like I didn't belong and now I realized it was just that I hadn't found my place yet. I hated the circumstances that brought me into Ray's life, but they were what they were. I wished every day Francis was alive, not a day went by I didn't miss him or want to show him something. I got solace in the fact justice was done, and his death brought Ray in and many more lives were saved. We were alive, living the best life we could, and loving every second of it.

THE END

ACKNOWLEDGMENTS

There are so many people we would like to thank for getting The Hunt out in the world. Our friends and family for sure because without them we likely would be in a cave somewhere rocking back and forth.

Thank you to our beta's Michele, Annabella, and Tracey. You are outstanding humans. To our editor, Steph, for not only making our words shine but for being our sanity. Thank you to Morningstar of Designs by Morningstar for our brilliant cover, and all the teasers we've had. Also, thank you to Michelle of Vibrant Promotions for guiding us in our promoting this crazy book. You're always a gem. Thank you finally to Melissa for being an epic proofreader and catching those last-minute gremlins. You all are priceless to us.

We very much want to thank you, our readers, for encouraging us, supporting us, and being the reason, we continue to do this. You leave us speechless with your awesomeness!

ABOUT DAVIDSON KING

Davidson King, always had a hope that someday her daydreams would become real-life stories. As a child, you would often find her in her own world, thinking up the most insane situations. It may have taken her awhile, but she made her dream come true with her first published work, Snow Falling.

When she's not writing you can find her blogging away on Diverse Reader, her review and promotional site. She managed to wrangle herself a husband who matched her crazy and they hatched three wonderful children.

If you were to ask her what gave her the courage to finally publish, she'd tell you it was her amazing family and friends. Support is vital in all things and when you're afraid of your dreams, it will be your cheering section that will lift you up.

ALSO BY DAVIDSON KING

Haven Hart Universe

Snow Falling

Hug It Out

A Dangerous Dance

ABOUT J.M. DABNEY

J.M. Dabney is a multi-genre author who writes mainly LGBT romance and fiction. They live with a constant diverse cast of characters in their head. No matter their size, shape, race, etc. they write for one purpose alone, and that's to make sure they do those characters justice and give them the happily ever after they deserve. J.M. is dysfunction at its finest and they make sure their characters are a beautiful kaleidoscope of crazy. There is nothing more they want from telling their stories than to show that no matter the package the characters come in or the damage their pasts have done, that love is love. That normal is never normal and sometimes the so-called broken can still be amazing.

ALSO BY J.M. DABNEY

Sappho's Kiss Series

When All Else Fails

More Than What They See

Dysfunction it its Finest Series

Club Revenge

Soul Collector Prophecy

Twirled World Ink Series

Berzerker

Trouble

Scary

Lucky

Brawlers Series

Crave

Psycho

Bull

Hunter

Executioners Series

Ghost

Joker

King

Sin & Saint

Trenton Security

Livingston

Little

Masiello Brothers

The Taming of Violet

3 Moments Trilogy

A Matter of Time

The Men of Canter's Handyman

Black Leather & Knuckle Tattoos

AUTHOR'S NOTE

Authors' Note

JM Dabney and Davidson King thank you for reading The Hunt. We had an awesome time writing it and we hoped you enjoyed it. If you have a moment, please feel free to review it and share your thoughts.

We love hearing from our readers and you can find us both in our facebook groups:

JM's group:

https://www.facebook.com/groups/585182991553194/

Davidson's Group:

https://www.facebook.com/groups/DavidsonKingsCourt/

Thank you so very much

CPSIA information can be obtained
at www.ICGtesting.com
Printed in the USA
LVHW080915131020
668643LV00028B/2467